THE PROBLEM WITH PELICANS

BY MS. MAUDIE LANCASTER

Part 1 of The Wahoo Bay Chronicles

LOCATIONS

Hillsboro Beach, Florida
Latitude: 26.2897 N Longitude: -80.0737 W

Located in Hillsboro Beach, Florida, this exclusive barrier island strip stretches for approximately 3.2 miles between the Atlantic Ocean and the Intracoastal Waterway. The unique geography provides residents with both oceanfront access and private docks. The strip runs north-south, with the Hillsboro Inlet Lighthouse & Wahoo Bay marking its southern terminus. Each estate spans from ocean to Intracoastal, allowing for the rare privilege of dual-water frontage. The area sits elevated on a natural dune system, providing protection from storm surge while offering commanding views of both waterways. Bridges connect properties across the Intracoastal to the mainland.

Wahoo Bay, Florida
Latitude: 26° 17' 22.80" N Longitude: -80° 04' 25.20" W

The protected inlet resonates with the gentle lapping of waves against weathered mangrove roots and the distinctive calls of brown pelicans. Salt-laden air mingles with the earthy scent of ancient mangroves, while sea spray creates rainbow prisms in the morning light. The water shifts from deep azure in the channel to crystalline turquoise in the shallows, where seagrass beds wave with each tide. At dawn and dusk, the iconic silhouette of the Hillsboro Lighthouse casts long shadows across the water, while pelicans glide silently overhead.

Andros Island, Bahamas
Latitude: 24.4333 N Longitude: -77.9500 W

Andros Island, nestled in the breathtaking expanse of The Bahamas, is a stunning paradise of vibrant colors and natural beauty. Its lush landscapes are adorned with swaying palm trees, while crystal-clear waters cascade into the pristine sandy beaches. The island boasts an array of rich ecosystems, from sprawling mangroves to vibrant coral reefs teeming with marine life.

1

LIFE IN PARADISE

As the morning sun peeked over the Atlantic Ocean, it threw long shards of light through the clouds that drifted over the wild Gulf Stream. Chip Waverly found himself reluctantly rolling out of bed, his feet hitting the cool floor as he shuffled barefoot to his second-story balcony. The blue Japanese roof tiles sparkled like precious gems under the bright Florida sky, a beauty that felt a little stifling sometimes.

Below him, the massive black lava-bottom pool seemed to spill into the seagrapes, which seamlessly rolled into the Atlantic. Hillsboro Mile stretched out before him like a shiny ribbon of wealth and privilege, each stunning house standing tall as a symbol of success. Yet, he couldn't shake the feeling that it was all just a show, a shiny cage that trapped him in a life he was starting to question.

At seventeen, Chip had a life that most kids could only dream about. He lived in this massive mansion that his grandparents had built back in the awesome 1980s, a place that really showed off their style and creativity. The house was funded by the profits from his great-great-grandfather, Thomas Waverly's amazing invention for trains and railways. It sat on a beautiful oceanfront acre, surrounded by the lush, vibrant greenery of Florida, where palm trees danced in the warm breeze and colorful flowers popped everywhere. The mansion had the best croquet lawn around, its grass a crisp emerald green, and perfect for fun games and laughter. Across busy A1A, two boats swayed gently on their moorings next to the immaculate tennis courts. One was his dad's sleek 27-foot center helm, ready for epic adventures on the water, while the other was Chip's absolute pride and joy: a 13' Mako 13 cc skiff. He had worked super hard to get this beauty, winning the South Florida Junior Fishing Championship three years in a row to earn it.

But still, there was this deep emptiness that wouldn't go away. No amount of money or trophies could fill that gap. Maybe it was just the weird feeling of not knowing what he was really supposed to do.

At only 17, he was stuck wrestling with these heavy thoughts, thoughts that felt way too intense to deal with, too "not cool" to think about. So, he picked up fishing, trying to find peace in the chill of just casting a line, even though part of him was craving something more, something he just couldn't grasp.

Chip snagged a pair of worn board shorts from his drawer, the fabric soft and faded from endless beach days. He threw on an old tournament tee, featuring the logo of a long-gone surf comp, the once-bright colors now kind of dull. Raking his fingers through his messy, sun-kissed hair, he caught a glance of himself in the mirror; it looked like he had just come out of the waves. But honestly, it was just a vibe, nothing carefree about him at the moment.

"Chip! Breakfast!" He heard his mother's lulling Knightsbridge accent floated through the air, a warm and inviting melody that echoed across the sprawling home from the kitchen. The rich tones of her voice, infused with the remnants of a British dialect, danced lightly around the sunlit rooms, a charming reminder of her years spent in the UK. Even after some years of living in Florida, she clung to her accent like a cherished heirloom, its familiar cadence wrapping around Chip like a cozy blanket on a cool morning.

Chip and his two sisters, Sloan and Willow, are lively new additions to Hillsboro Mile from New York. Their mother, Emila, a spirited American fashion buyer with Harrod's, and their father, Liam, who grew up in this very home, but chose to relocate to New York to pursue a career in finance. Even so, he always kept his identity as an avid surfer and diver, and after many years away, decided to move his family back to his beloved Florida. His brother, Marcus, was already based on The Mile. He has a family with two sons, Jake and Tanner, and a wife named Kim.

The NYC Waverly's would retreat every summer to their family's grand mansion that overlooked the ocean, where the salty air mingled with the sounds of waves crashing nearby. The children relished the long, sun-soaked days spent with their cousins, the FL Waverly's, especially Jake and Tanner, who lived at the end of the Mile near the Hillsboro Lighthouse. Over the years, those summer gatherings strengthened their bond, transforming them into more than just relatives; they became best friends, united by shared memories and laughter that echoed along the sandy shores. Chip was still amazed that his parents decided to move the family back to Florida and their original home.

The kitchen was a clean and modern area with a blend of sueded granite and enameled appliances, featuring floor-to-ceiling windows that provided a clear view of the Atlantic Ocean. Emilia Waverly stood at the grand island, meticulously arranging fresh fruit on a platter with the skill of a surgeon.

At forty-five, she flowed through the home like the shiny trend setter she had always been, even before she married into the Waverly wealth. Her glossy dark hair was cut into a sleek espresso brown bob, and she donned a relaxed linen jumper straight from the Goop catalogue.

"Morning, Mom," Chip said, grabbing a piece of mango from the platter.

"Your father's already left for the office," she said, her voice tinged with a hint of exasperation. "He mentioned something about the Tokyo markets opening early. You know how he becomes when those numbers start swirling and dancing in his head, like a whirlwind of figures and charts that he can't resist chasing after."

Chip nodded in agreement, albeit somewhat hesitantly. Liam Waverly was a man who lived and breathed finance, navigating the tumultuous waters of global markets with the same fervor and passion that Chip applied to the actual waves of the ocean. The Waverly wealth, a towering testament to ambition, had been meticulously crafted from the groundbreaking invention of the modern rail track coupler by Liam's great-grandfather, Thomas. The Waverly estate is the capstone to Hillsboro Mile, an exclusive strip of land where Broward's elite watch the Atlantic Ocean lapping at their front yard and the Intracoastal meandering in the back. The enclave contains five of the country's ten most expensive homes.

They were hard working, tremendously generous people. They did not play in a lot of the players' circles, which would be what is expected from them. Fortuitously for their family, it was Henry Flagler who spearheaded the construction of the new railroad, utilizing Thomas Waverly's invention and forever transforming the landscape of Florida. That ingenious invention had continued to yield dividends daily, a legacy of prosperity that echoed through time since its very first implementation. With that legacy, the Waverly's had been a staple on the mile for three generations.

"Where are the girls?" Chip asked, referring to his sisters, Sloan and Willow.

"Sloan's already at the lab," Emilia replied. "She said something about a breakthrough in her research that couldn't wait. And Willow..." she paused, a slight frown creasing her brow. "Willow is trying to become an influencer for the City of Miami Beach and had a late night. But with 500k followers, she's doing something right."

Chip's sisters were as different as night and day, but not when it comes to brains and hard work. Sloan, twenty-one, was a certified genius who'd graduated from MIT at nineteen and was now pursuing her doctorate in marine biology at the University of

Miami. She spent most of her time either in the lab or diving in the waters around South Florida, studying coral reef ecosystems with an intensity that bordered on obsession.

Willow, nineteen, had taken a different path entirely. Both sisters had luminous charm, along with their mother's glossy brown hair, but where Sloan collected degrees, Willow collected experiences, and had decided to create a company that helped people achieve their own dream experiences. She was currently "taking a gap year" that had stretched into two years, in order to become an influencer. She became so popular in such a short time that F1 races, Design District openings, and exclusive parties that lasted until dawn had to wait in line for her response to attend.

"I'm going to check on the boats," Chip said, grabbing a banana and heading for the door.

"Don't forget you have that appointment with your college counselor this afternoon," his mother called after him.

Chip's steps faltered slightly, like he had stepped onto a rickety old floating dock. The college counselor, another reminder of the future that everyone expected him to embrace. Harvard, Yale, Princeton, even Oxford - the Ivy League schools were practically lining up to recruit him, not just for his athletic abilities, but for his family name and the generous donations that would undoubtedly follow. But the thought of four more years of structured education, of following a predetermined path, was just too ick to think about.

The morning air was thick with humidity, but the water was clear to the bottom in the Intracoastal waterway. This always put a smile on his face, no matter what the world presented him. Chip traced along the narrow concrete walkway that encircled the waterfront tennis court across A1A to the moorings where the boats almost swirled on their ropes like drunk tourists after a night at the Elbo Room. He loved this time of day, before the heat became oppressive, and the waterway filled with weekend warriors and tourists.

A great blue heron stood motionless at the end of the dock, its yellow eyes fixed on that clear water below.

As he checked the lines on his boat, his phone vibrated with a text from his cousin Jake: "Dude, you need to see this. Meet me at Cap's Place in 20. And bring snacks. I'm starving."

Jake and his younger brother, Tanner, resided a short distance down the Mile, in a house that, while not quite as grand as Chip's, still boasted an air of elegance and sophistication. Their father, Marcus Waverly, was the younger sibling of Chip's father, and he had carved out his own prosperous empire in the realms of construction and real estate development. While Liam immersed himself in the world of abstract numbers and the ebb and flow of market trends, Marcus thrived in the tangible realm of concrete and steel, skillfully transforming barren lots into opulent luxury developments that dotted the vibrant landscape of South Florida. Each project bore his signature touch, a testament to his vision and ambition, as he reshaped the very shoreline with his relentless drive and expertise.

Chip grabbed some snacks and water from the under counter refrigerator inside the tiki hut that doubled as the "clubhouse" for the tennis court. He lowered the dreamy little Mako, fired up his single engine, and headed south to Hillsboro Inlet along the Intracoastal, the 40hp outboard purring smoothly as he navigated the familiar waters. The morning was perfect for boating: glassy, light wind, and visibility that stretched for miles. He passed the usual collection of mega-yachts and sport fishers lining the seawall, their crews already preparing for a day on the water.

Cap's Place was a small restaurant from 1928. Along with being a restaurant, it was a speakeasy and gambling den for rum runners and sea fairing kind. Being the oldest extant structure in the City of Lighthouse Point and the oldest commercial enterprise in the area, it was always exciting to visit to the boys. It sat on a spit of land with a mini-beach that jutted into the Intracoastal about halfway between the two houses. It had been their secret meeting place since they were kids, as it was their parents as well. It's accessible only by boat or by a treacherous scramble through the mangroves.

Jake was already waiting when Chip showed up, his boat tied to a driftwood log along the small beach in the shallow water. Cap's security team, a group of wild yet amiable cats, were wandering around the property, and one of them familiar with the boys, approached Chip to see if there were any morning treats.

"Check this out," Jake said without preamble.

At nineteen, Jake had inherited the Waverly height and athletic build, but where Chip was all smooth confidence, Jake had a nervous energy that kept him constantly in motion. His thick, dark hair was perpetually messy, and he had a habit of pushing his hair out of his face when he was excited, which he was doing now.

His brother, Tanner, sixteen, with his shaggy light brown hair, was the one that watched over them both. Not as tall as Jake, but strong as him, and could fully keep up, if not compete, with Chip.

"What am I looking at?" Chip asked, squinting at the phone screen.

"Aerial photos of Wahoo Bay Island," Jake said.

"Look at this one from last month, and then this one from yesterday."

Chip studied the images. Wahoo Bay Island was part of the Hillsboro Inlet, about two miles south of their houses, at the base of the Hillsboro Lighthouse and the Hillsboro Inlet bridge. A small triangular island of pristine land on the west side of the bridge, along A1A, that had remained undeveloped for as long as he could remember. In the first photo, he could see the familiar tangle of Spanish Pines and mangroves and the small parcel of land where pelicans had nested for generations. In the second photo, virtually overnight, half of the pines were gone, replaced by raw earth and construction equipment.

"Someone's building there," Chip said, though even as he said it, something felt wrong. "But I thought that was protected land."

"That's what I thought too." Jake said, "So I did some digging. Guess who just pulled permits for a luxury condo development on Wahoo Bay Island?"

Chip felt a cold knot form in his stomach. "Please don't tell me."

"Waverly Construction," Tanner chimed in and said grimly. "My dad is bulldozing the pelican sanctuary. Apparently, yesterday a pelican dive-bombed the construction foreman's lunch."

Despite everything, Chip couldn't help but crack a smile. "Well, at least the pelicans are fighting back."

"Right? Nature's revenge," Jake said. "Though I'm pretty sure that's not going to stop our dad from turning their home into 'The Gilded Nest' Luxury Condominiums or whatever ridiculous name he comes up with."

The words hit Chip like a ton of bricks. He'd had summer after summer growing up with Jake and Tanner watching the pelicans at Wahoo Bay, and had learned to identify different species during countless trips in and out of the inlet with his father. The sanctuary wasn't just a piece of land, it was a living ecosystem that had existed since the bridge was built.

"There has to be some mistake," Chip said, but even as he spoke, he remembered his uncle's recent behavior. Marcus had been unusually secretive lately, taking phone calls in private and deflecting questions about his current projects. During the most recent family dinner, he appeared to be out of sorts, and oddly declined to have his favorite shrimp cocktail at Houston's.

"I tried looking up information about the sanctuary online," Jake continued, "but here's the weird part, there's almost nothing there. Like, nothing. No environmental impact studies, no historical records, no mention of it being protected land. It's like someone scrubbed the internet clean with a magic eraser."

Chip stared at the photos again, his mind racing.

The pelican sanctuary at Wahoo Bay had been a constant in his life, as permanent and unchanging as the tides themselves. The idea that it could simply be erased, bulldozed away for another luxury development, filled him with a rage he'd never experienced before.

"We have to do something," he said finally, dramatically placing his hand over his heart.

"Like what? It's my dad's company. Our family's company. Plus, you know how scary he gets," Tanner said.

"I don't care whose company it is," Chip said, his voice harder than he'd intended. "This is wrong."

Jake studied his cousin's face, recognizing the expression he'd seen countless times before competitions. When Chip got that look, when his jaw set in that particular way, nothing could stop him.

"Okay," Jake said slowly. "What do you want to do?"

"First, we must uncover the truth behind the catastrophic loss of all that vital information online. No one simply misplaces decades of environmental records without a sinister motive lurking beneath the surface. And second, we must expose the exact details of Uncle Marcus's grand scheme for that land. What is he truly plotting to unleash upon the pelican sanctuary?"

"And third?" Tanner asked.

Chip looked out across the water toward Wahoo Bay Island, where construction equipment was already scarring the landscape.

"Third," Chip said, "we stop him."

2

THE INVESTIGATION BEGINS

Later that afternoon, Chip sat in the college counselor's office, nodding at appropriate intervals while Mrs. Henderson discussed his "intelligence for his young age," "bright future," and "unlimited potential."

The words washed over him like white noise as his mind kept returning every few minutes to the aerial photos Jake had shown him. He found himself checking his phone, hoping for updates from his cousin.

"Chip? Are you listening?" Mrs. Henderson's

voice cut through his distraction, along with the sound of her stress ball squeaking ominously.

"Sorry, yes. Harvard. Great opportunity. Totally not me, but good." He forced himself to focus on the woman across from him, with her perfectly styled gray hair and collection of motivational posters that seemed to be judging him personally.

"I was saying that with your athletic achievements and family connections, you could have your pick of schools. But you need to start thinking seriously about what you want to study. What interests you?"

The question hung in the air between them. What interested him? A week ago, he might have said, "I just want to be a fisherman, or a businessman like my father." But sitting there, thinking about the pelican sanctuary being destroyed, he realized he'd never been asked what he actually cared about.

"Environmental science and maybe a Blue Economy major," he said suddenly, surprising himself.

Blue Economy was a relatively new term that he learned from his sister, Sloan, because of her research. This umbrella covers subjects that involve Marine Research and Education (research stations, educational programs, scientific partnerships), Conservation Technology (artificial reef development, marine habitat restoration), Sustainable Tourism (eco-tours, cultural education programs, research tourism), Environmental Consulting (international advisory services, conservation planning), and Sustainable Fishing (managed fishing grounds, artificial reef systems).

Mrs. Henderson raised an eyebrow and nearly choked on her coffee. "That's, unexpected. What sparked this interest? Did you have some kind of nature documentary marathon or watch Shark Week?"

Chip thought about how to explain without revealing too much. "I spend a lot of time on the water. I've started noticing changes in the ecosystem, things that don't seem right."

It wasn't entirely true, but it wasn't entirely false either. As he uttered the words, a strange sensation washed over him, as if those syllables were woven with threads of sincerity, more genuine than anything he'd expressed about his future in months. The weight of his confession settled in the air, and for the first time in a long while, he felt a flicker of clarity, like a beam of sunlight breaking through the clouds of uncertainty that had enveloped him for so long.

"Well, that's wonderfully specific," said Mrs. Henderson, making notes on her tablet.

He went on to explain to her that these industries create a synergistic network where each sector supports and enhances the others, creating multiple revenue streams from single conservation initiatives.

"There are some excellent programs. Scripps has a fantastic marine and environmental science department, and of course, Stanford's environmental engineering program is world-renowned."

They spent the next thirty minutes discussing course requirements and application deadlines, but Chip's heart wasn't in it. The college opportunities felt out of touch with what Chip already knew. It was like a distant concern compared to what was happening at Wahoo Bay.

When he finally escaped the counselor's office, he found Jake and Tanner waiting by his truck in the school parking lot.

Tanner, at sixteen, was the youngest of the three cousins but often the most level-headed. Where Jake was all nervous energy and dramatic gestures, Tanner had inherited their grandfather's calm, analytical nature and dark blue eyes.

"Please tell me you found something," Chip said with no formalities of a hello.

"Oh, we found something all right," Tanner said, holding up a manila folder. "But you're not going to like it."

They drove to a small diner on Ft. Lauderdale beach, far enough from Hillsboro Mile that they wouldn't run into anyone they knew. The afternoon crowd was thin, mostly retirees and a few tourists studying maps and guidebooks like they were deciphering ancient hieroglyphics.

"Okay, here's what we know," Jake said, spreading papers across their corner table with the dramatic flair of a detective in a bad TV show. "The land at Wahoo Bay has been in some kind of legal limbo for decades. Officially, it's owned by a shell company called GenCoast Properties LLC."

"And unofficially?" Chip asked, stealing one of Tanner's fries.

"Unofficially," Jake said. "GenCoast Properties is owned by another shell company, which is owned by another shell company. But luckily, Tanner here is a wizard with public records searches."

Tanner pushed his hair out of his face, a gesture he'd picked up from his brother from Jake. "I traced it back through six different companies. The ultimate owner is Waverly Construction, but they've been very careful to hide that connection."

"So my uncle definitely owns it," Chip thought to himself.

"It gets worse," Tanner continued, "I found the original environmental impact study from 1987. The land was supposed to be permanently protected as a pelican nesting sanctuary. But somehow, that designation was quietly removed in 2020, during COVID, when people were very distracted and no one would notice."

"How does something like that just get removed?" Chip asked.

"Money," Jake said grimly. "Lots of money, and the right connections."

Tanner pulled out another document. "This is the current development plan. They're calling it 'Pelican Pointe,' note the pretentious spelling. Eight luxury condos, starting at three million each." The irony of naming the development after the pelicans, while reports of pelican attacks on the construction crew had now climbed to 6, was not lost on the Waverly boys.

Chip studied the architectural renderings, his anger growing with each page. The development was small, but it covered every inch of the pelican sanctuary. Where ancient mangroves and shade-giving pines had provided nesting sites for generations of pelicans, there would be swimming pools and tennis courts. Where shallow waters had teemed with fish and crustaceans, there would be private docks for yachts and jet skis. Chip had nothing against yachts and jet skis. They were, in fact, a part of his everyday life, but there were much better places to put them, places where they belong, and they certainly didn't belong at Wahoo Bay Island.

"There's something else," Tanner said quietly, "I found some old newspaper articles from the 1920s. Before it was a pelican sanctuary, Wahoo Bay Island was considered a sacred island by the Miccosukee tribe."

"Sacred how?" Chip asked.

"Burial ground. The articles mention that several tribal elders warned against any development on the island, saying it would bring bad luck to anyone who disturbed it."

Jake snorted, nearly choking on his drink. "Come on, Tanner. You don't actually believe in ancient curses."

"I don't know what I believe," Tanner said. "But I know that every attempt to develop that land over the past century has ended in disaster. In 1933, a hotel developer went bankrupt after his construction crew was hit by three hurricanes in one season. In 1954, a shopping center developer died in a car accident the day after breaking ground. In 1978, a marina developer's entire project was destroyed by a sinkhole that opened up overnight."

"Coincidences," Jake said, but his voice lacked conviction.

"Maybe," Tanner said, "but the Miccosukee tribe still considers that island sacred. I found a quote from a tribal elder in a 1987 newspaper article: 'The spirits of our ancestors rest in that place. To disturb them is to invite their anger, not just on the one who does the disturbing, but on all who benefit from it.'"

Chip felt a chill despite the warm afternoon air.

He'd grown up hearing stories about the Miccosukee tribe, whose ancestors had lived in South Florida for thousands of years before the first European settlers arrived. Their connection to the land ran deeper than property deeds and development rights. Their legal team was even stronger. They went up against the state of Florida and won several times. This will be a fight that they could win.

"We need to talk to them," he said suddenly!

"Talk to who?" Jake asked.

"The Miccosukee. If this land is really sacred to them, they have a right to know what's happening. And maybe they can help us stop it."

"How exactly do we contact a Native American tribe?" Tanner asked, "There's not exactly an 'Ancient Curse Consultants' office next to Publix."

"Actually," Chip said, pulling out his phone, "I might know someone who can help."

He remembered Dr. Sarah Blackwater, who had been Sloan's research advisor at UM. She was also a member of the Miccosukee tribe and one of the leading experts on South Florida's indigenous history and legalese. He quickly scrolled through the University website, and found her direct line, immediately dialing it.

"Dr. Blackwater? This is Chip Waverly, Sloan's brother. Yes, she's doing great, listen, I need to ask you about something, and I hope you won't think I'm crazy."

He explained the situation as clearly as he could, from the destruction of the pelican sanctuary to the historical significance of the land. Dr. Blackwater listened without interruption, occasionally asking for clarification at his descriptions of the pelican uprising.

"You're not crazy, Chip," she said finally. "That land has been sacred sanctuary for the brown pelican for generations. We've been fighting to protect it for decades, but we don't have the legal standing to challenge development permits. Though I have to say, the pelicans seem to be doing a better job than our lawyers."

"What would it take to stop the construction?" Chip asked.

"Proof that the permits were obtained illegally, or evidence of significant environmental damage. But even then, it would be an uphill battle. Your uncle has a lot of political connections."

"What about the curse?" Chip asked. Many locals knew about it as well.

Dr. Blackwater was quiet for a long moment. "My grandmother used to say that the land itself has a memory. It remembers those who were kind and considerate to it. It also remembers every slight, and every act of disrespect. Whether you call it a curse or simply the natural consequences of disturbing a delicate ecosystem, bad things do tend to happen to those who harm sacred places."

"Would you be willing to meet with us? To tell us more about the history of the land?"

"I'll do better than that," Dr. Blackwater said. "I'll arrange for you to meet with some of the tribal elders. But I have to warn you, they're not going to be happy about what's happening at Wahoo Bay."

After hanging up, Chip looked at his cousins and dramatically threw himself back in his chair. "We're meeting with the tribal elders tomorrow evening."

"This is really happening, isn't it?" Jake said. "We're really going to take on our own family?!?"

"We're going to try to save the sanctuary," Chip corrected. "If that means taking them on, then so be it."

Tanner gathered up the papers. He carefully slid them back into the folder, but not before doing a little victory dance in his seat. "There's one more thing we should probably consider."

"What's that?"

"If we're right about this being some kind of cover up, then our own father, your uncle, went to a lot of trouble to hide the truth about that land. And he's not going to be happy when we start digging around."

Chip thought about the scrubbed internet records, the shell companies, the quietly removed environmental protections. Tanner was right, this wasn't just a simple development project. Marcus had invested serious time and money in making sure the truth about Wahoo Bay stayed buried.

"Then we'll have to be careful," he said, but hey, at least we'll have the pelicans on our side."

As they stepped out of the diner, Chip was engulfed by a surge of emotion he hadn't felt in ages: an electrifying sense of purpose that coursed through his veins like a tidal wave. The nagging thought that had tormented him finally crystallized into a fierce determination.

For the first time in his existence, he was engaged in a battle that transcended the hollow victories of trophies, or the suffocating weight of each college application, and the crushing expectations of family. The pelican sanctuary on Wahoo Bay Island may have been on the brink of annihilation, but the ferocious struggle to protect what little remained had only just ignited.

3

SECRETS AND REVELATIONS

The following morning ushered in the best weather South Florida has to offer: pristine blue skies, a soft breeze, and temperatures that lingered in the ideal range that allow you to wear actual clothing without melting.

Chip was up before dawn, unable to sleep with everything that was racing through his mind. He'd spent most of the night researching environmental law and indigenous rights, as well as family entitlements, trying to understand what legal options they might have.

He found his sister, Sloan, in the kitchen, already dressed in her diving gear and packing equipment into a waterproof bag. Her dark hair was pulled back in a smooth ponytail, and she moved with the efficient precision of someone who'd done this routine hundreds of times.

"Early dive today?" Chip asked, while pouring himself a bowl of cereal and then experiencing the everlasting struggle to immediately reopen the fridge door after forgetting the blueberries.

"Coral bleaching survey off Virginia Key," Sloan replied without looking up, somehow managing to stuff what looked like half of a dive shop into her bag. "The water temperatures have been abnormally high this summer, and we're seeing massive die-offs in the reef systems. Plus, I may have accidentally promised to bring back samples for three different research projects."

Chip watched his sister work, struck by how she could make environmental disaster sound like a casual Tuesday. Sloan had always been driven, but her dedication to marine conservation bordered on obsession, the kind where she had a personalized shark plate that read "blackfin" on her new, blue Rivian.

"Sloan," he said carefully, "what do you know about the pelican sanctuary at Wahoo Bay?"

His sister's hands stilled on her equipment bag.

"Why do you ask? And please tell me you didn't try to pet one of the pelicans again."

"Just curious. I was out there yesterday and noticed construction. Also, I learned my lesson about pelican beaks when I was twelve."

Sloan turned to face him, her expression serious. "Chip, that sanctuary has been protected for decades. There shouldn't be any construction there."

"That's what I thought too." He pulled out his phone and showed her the aerial photos Jake had taken. "But look at this."

Sloan studied the images, her face growing pale. "This is impossible. The environmental protections on that island are ironclad. I wrote my undergraduate thesis on that ecosystem. I spent so much time there that the pelicans started recognizing me."

"You wrote about Wahoo Bay Island?" Chip asked.

"It's one of the most important pelican nesting sites in South Florida. The mangrove system of the island supports dozens of species. The Spanish pine and the shallow waters are a crucial nursery habitat for juvenile fish." She sank into a chair, nearly sitting on a diving weight.

She shook her head, refocusing on the photos. "But who's doing this construction?"

Chip paused, a flicker of uncertainty crossing his face. He had wished to shield the family connection from the unfolding chaos, at least until he grasped the full scope of what was happening around him. The air was thick with tension, and the weight of unspoken words hung heavily between them. But as he contemplated the situation, he realized that Sloan deserved to hear the truth, no matter how difficult it might be. After all, she was astute and perceptive; she would likely piece together the puzzle on her own, regardless.

"Waverly Construction," he said quietly.

The color drained completely from Sloan's face. "Uncle Marcus? But that's…he wouldn't, he knows how important that sanctuary is. I literally cornered him at last year's Christmas party and made him listen to my twenty-minute presentation about mangrove ecosystems."

"Are you sure he was listening? Maybe he was just nodding politely," Chip said.

Sloan sat in silence, her brow furrowed as her analytical mind whirred with activity, sifting through the intricacies and far-reaching implications of the information before her. The stillness around her seemed to amplify her thoughts, each one tumbling over the other like a cascade of ideas, as she weighed the significance of what she had just learned.

"There's something you need to see," she said finally.

Chip followed Sloan to the living room, then up the curved staircase to her room. Willow's room was directly across. Sloan's room resembled a bustling research laboratory more than a traditional bedroom. The walls were adorned with a vibrant collage of charts detailing the intricate patterns of ocean currents, interspersed with graphs that tracked shifts in water temperature. The room was alive with images of coral reefs, showcasing their stunning beauty in various stages of decay, each photograph telling a story of the fragile underwater world.

Her desk, though, was a tidy treasure trove, neatly stacked with scientific journals and research papers, the surface was clear glass over the wood desktop. Atop this mountain of knowledge sat a large, weathered chunk of coral, its rough texture and faded colors serving as a stubborn paperweight, a tangible reminder of the ocean's mysteries and the urgent need to protect them.

"I've been tracking environmental changes along the South Florida coast for the past two years," she said, pulling out a thick binder. "Water quality, fish populations, nesting bird counts, coral health, everything."

She opened the binder to a section marked "Wahoo Bay Island," and spread out a series of charts and graphs. "Look at this data from the pelican sanctuary. For the past fifty years, it's been one of the most stable ecosystems in the region. Consistent nesting populations, healthy fish stocks, excellent water quality."

"And now?" Chip asked.

Sloan went on to now describe what's happening at Wahoo Bay. "Starting about six months ago, everything began to change. Fish populations dropped by thirty percent. Water quality declined significantly. And the pelican nesting numbers," she pointed to a graph that showed a dramatic downward trend while doing an exaggerated sad face. "They're down by almost sixty percent from last year."

Chip studied the data, trying to understand what he was seeing. "What could cause changes like that?"

"Pollution, habitat disruption, changes in water flow patterns." Sloan's voice was grim. "The kind of changes you'd see if someone was doing preliminary work for a major construction project."

Sloan began to describe another situation that had unfolded. "In a remote coastal region, the tranquility of the habitat was shattered when developers began their covert operations. They didn't rely on bulldozers or heavy machinery; instead, they employed a more insidious approach. Through the introduction of invasive species, they altered the delicate balance of the local ecosystem. These foreign plants and animals thrived, out-competing native species for resources, slowly choking the life out of the indigenous flora and fauna. The vibrant wetlands, once teeming with diverse wildlife, began to succumb to this silent invasion.

As the developers continued their scheme, they discreetly drained the marshes to provide easier access for construction, unknowingly unleashing a chain reaction that destabilized the entire area. The once bustling habitat grew quieter, with fewer birds returning to their nesting grounds and fish populations dwindling. Without a single bulldozer in sight, the ecological damage was profound, illustrating how the slow, calculated sabotage of an environment can lay waste to the natural world, leaving scars that may take decades to heal."

Chip stood listening in amazement."You think Uncle Marcus has been working on this for months?"

"I suspected that someone has been methodically dismantling that delicate ecosystem, likely in an effort to downplay the environmental impact assessment when they eventually seek permits. Never in my wildest dreams did I think it would be my own uncle. The vibrant tapestry of life that once thrived here is now suffering, and honestly? The local wildlife is visibly distressed, their habitats disrupted and their survival threatened."

The implications hit Chip like a physical blow. This wasn't just about building condos on protected land, it was about deliberately sabotaging an entire ecosystem to make the development seem less harmful.

"Sloan, we have to stop this."

His sister looked at him with a mixture of admiration and concern, while straightening a photo of Jacques Cousteau. "Chip, I've been trying to study environmental destruction my entire educational life. It's not as simple as just wanting to do the right thing. There are legal processes, regulatory agencies, political considerations. Most of all, what will this do to Uncle Marcus, our family?"

"What if we could prove that the permits were obtained illegally? Or that the environmental impact was deliberately understated?"

Sloan was quiet for a moment, her analytical mind working through the possibilities while she fiddled with a stress ball shaped like a sea turtle. "It would take more than just my data. We'd need documentation of the permit process, evidence of deliberate environmental sabotage, probably testimony from environmental experts."

"What about the Miccosukee tribe? The land is sacred to them."

"That could be significant," Sloan said slowly. "There are federal laws protecting Native American sacred sites. But proving the connection would be complicated."

Chip's phone buzzed with a text from Jake: "Emergency. Meet at Cap's ASAP!"

"I have to go," Chip said, helping Sloan gather up the photos and data. "But Sloan, I need your help with this. Your research could be the key to stopping the development."

His sister studied his face, seeing something there she'd never noticed before.

"You're truly committed to this, aren't you?"

"More serious than I've ever been about anything."

Sloan nodded slowly, grinning. "Okay. But we do this right. No cool guy heroics, no breaking the law, and no discussing with our parents yet. We get the facts, and use scientific and legal channels to build a case."

"Agreed," Chip said, though privately he wondered if legal channels would be enough to stop what was happening at Wahoo Bay Island.

A few minutes later, he was racing down the Intracoastal towards Cap's Place, his boat's engine pushed to its legal limit.

Jake's text had been uncharacteristically urgent, and Chip could see his cousins' boat already anchored in the shallow water.

"What's the emergency?" he called out as he pulled alongside Jake's boat, nearly ramming into it in the process.

"We went back to Wahoo Bay this morning to

get more photos," Tanner said, his face pale. "But we weren't the only ones there."

"What do you mean?"

Jake held up his phone, showing a video he'd recorded. "We were about a quarter mile away when we saw this."

The video showed the construction site at Wahoo Bay, but now there were people moving around the equipment. Not just construction workers, these people were wearing suits and carrying briefcases. In the background, a large pelican could be seen circling overhead.

"Who are they?" Chip asked.

"Watch this part," Tanner said. The video showed the construction foreman sitting on a piece of equipment, the pelican swooped down and landed on the gears, nearly sending the foreman and the equipment into the Intracoastal!

"We got close enough to hear some of their conversation after the pelican incident," Tanner said. "They were talking about 'accelerating the timeline' and 'dealing with potential complications.' The foreman kept complaining about needing hazard pay for bird attacks."

"What kind of complications?"

"The kind that ask too many questions," Jake said. "Chip, I think they know we've been investigating. Though honestly, after watching that guy get dive-bombed by a pelican, I'm starting to think Mother Nature's on our side."

A chill ran down Chip's spine. "How could they know?"

"Consider this," Tanner urged, his voice low and charged with urgency. "You reached out to Dr. Blackwater just yesterday. I've been diving deep into public records, unearthing every detail. Jake's been snapping shots of the construction site like a hawk. If anyone's been keeping tabs on what's unfolding, they'd be keenly aware of the heightened scrutiny surrounding the project."

"So what do we do?"

"We could back off," Jake suggested, his voice barely above a whisper, as if the very trees might be listening. He glanced nervously over his shoulder, the tension in his shoulders taut like a drawn bow. "Pretend we never saw anything."

"No," Chip said firmly. "We're meeting with the tribal elders tonight. We're going to find out the truth about this land, and then we're going to stop whatever's happening there."

"Even if it's dangerous?" Tanner asked, his voice tinged with concern.

Chip turned his gaze out across the shimmering water toward Wahoo Bay, where massive construction equipment rumbled ominously on the island, its metal jaws tearing into the earth with a relentless, mechanical growl, leaving chaos in its wake.

"Especially if it's dangerous," Chip replied, his tone steady, as the sun glinted off the disturbed surface of the bay, casting fleeting reflections of a beauty that felt increasingly threatened.

4

THE ELDERS SPEAK

The Miccosukee Cultural Center was nestled on the cusp of the vast Everglades, its low-slung structure seamlessly blending with the lush greenery and the murmur of the swamp. The building, constructed from rustic wood, and adorned with intricate carvings, appeared to rise naturally from the earth, as if it had sprouted from the very soil itself. As the sun dipped toward the horizon, casting golden rays through the thick canopy of cypress trees, Chip, Jake, and Tanner made their way toward the entrance. The air was heavy with the scent of damp earth and wildflowers, and the distant call of birds echoed around them, creating an almost magical ambiance as they ventured into the heart of the Miccosukee heritage.

Dr. Sarah Blackwater met them at the door, her silver hair braided with colorful beads, and her dark eyes twinkling with joy as the boys entered. She was a small woman, probably in her sixties, but she carried herself with the quiet authority of someone who had spent decades fighting for her people's rights.

"Thank you for coming," she said, leading them through a hallway lined with historical photographs and traditional artwork. "The elders are very concerned about what's happening at Wahoo Bay."

The trio stepped into a spacious, circular, wood-paneled room, filled with fragrant scents of rich earth and history. Five elderly Miccosukee sat in a semi-circle. Their weathered faces, etched with lines of wisdom and experience, seemed to tell stories of generations past. They were dressed in surprisingly casual clothes, in comparison to the walls around them that were a tapestry of colors, adorned with intricate beadwork that glimmered softly under the warm light, and paintings that vividly captured the essence of South Florida's natural beauty. Alligators lurked in the murky waters, flamboyant birds took flight, and schools of fish darted through the lush greenery, all framed by the sprawling, verdant expanse of the Everglades.

"This is Chip Waverly and his cousins, Jake and Tanner," Dr. Blackwater said in both English and Miccosukee. "They're the ones who contacted me about the sacred land."

The eldest of the group, a man whose face suggested he was in his eighties, studied the boys with deep-set eyes that had undoubtedly witnessed the unfolding of Florida's rich history. Each wrinkle on his skin told a story, and his gaze was both piercing and contemplative, as if viewing a world long past. When he finally spoke, his voice emerged like a gentle breeze, soft yet imbued with the profound weight of countless decades, resonating with wisdom and the echoes of time.

"I am Joseph Osceola," he said. "My great-great-grandfather was one of the last to be buried on the island at Wahoo Bay, before the white man's government forced us to move deeper into the Everglades."

"We're honored to meet you," Chip said.

"Dr. Blackwater tells us that your family is responsible for the destruction of our sacred land," another elder said, her voice sharp with anger.

"My uncle's company, Jake and Tanner's father, is doing the construction," Chip admitted, "but I'm here because we want to stop it."

"Why?" Joseph Osceola asked. "Why would you go against your own family?"

Chip pondered the weight of the question, searching for the right words to express the depth of his conviction. He felt a fire ignite within him, a sense of urgency that pushed him to speak. "Because some things transcend family loyalty. This land isn't merely a piece of property owned by my uncle or any other profit-driven developer. It is a sacred sanctuary that belongs to the pelicans, who depend on it for their survival, and to your ancestors, who revered this ground long before we walked upon it. It is also a legacy for the future generations, who deserve to inherit a world rich in nature and heritage. This is about preserving something invaluable, something that connects us all. The land is a thread that ties past, present, and future together, and I cannot stand by while it is threatened."

The elders exchanged glances, communicating in their native language.

"Sit," Joseph Osceola said, gesturing to cushions arranged in a circle. "We will tell you the true history of that place."

For the next hour, the elders shared stories that had been passed down through generations. They spoke of Wahoo Bay as a place where the boundary between the physical and spiritual worlds was thin, where their ancestors had gone to communicate with the spirits of the dead. They described elaborate burial ceremonies conducted on the small spit of island, where tribal leaders had been laid to rest with artifacts that connected them to the natural world.

"The pelicans came later," Joseph Osceola explained. "After we were forced to leave, the birds made their nests where our ancestors sleep. We saw this as a sign, the spirits of our people were protecting the sacred land through the birds. Though I must say, I hear they're quite enthusiastic protectors."

"What happens if the construction continues?" Tanner asked.

The elders grew quiet, though their expressions seemed troubled now. Finally, Mary Tiger spoke.

"The spirits of the disturbed dead do not rest easy," she said solemnly, then added with a slight smirk, "and apparently, neither do their feathered guardians. They will seek justice, not just against those who harm the sacred land, but against all who profit from its destruction. Expect more animal incidents."

"You mean the curse is real?" Jake asked, his skepticism evident.

"Call it what you will," Joseph Osceola said, "but the land remembers, and the spirits of our ancestors are not powerless, or are they?"

Dr. Blackwater leaned forward. "From a legal standpoint, we may have grounds to challenge the development under the Native American Graves Protection and Repatriation Act. If we can prove that the island contains unmarked graves, federal law requires that construction be halted."

"How do we prove that?" Chip asked, his brow furrowed in concern. The weight of the discovery pressed heavily upon him; he understood that this wasn't just about uncovering the past, but about preserving it for future generations.

"Archaeological survey," she replied, her voice steady yet urgent, "but it would have to be done before the construction destroys any remaining evidence." Chip felt a surge of anxiety at the thought of losing invaluable artifacts to the relentless march of progress. Every layer of soil held stories waiting to be told, histories that could illuminate their understanding of the world. The urgency of the task loomed large in his mind, amplifying his determination to ensure that what lay beneath the surface would not be forgotten forever.

"The bulldozers are working around the clock," Jake said. "By the time we could arrange an official survey, there might be nothing left to find."

Joseph Osceola stood slowly, his joints creaking with age like an old ship. He walked to a cabinet and returned with a leather pouch, from which he withdrew several objects: arrowheads, pottery shards, and what looked like carved bone ornaments. A small gecko scurried across the table, apparently unimpressed by the ancient artifacts.

"These were found on the island by my great-grandfather in 1923," he said, gently shooing the gecko away, "before the government made it illegal for us to visit our sacred places. They are proof that our people lived and died on that island."

"Would these be enough evidence for a legal challenge?" Chip asked Dr. Blackwater.

"Possibly. But we'd need more than just artifacts. We'd need documentation of their provenance, expert authentication, and preferably some kind of ground-penetrating radar survey to locate actual burial sites."

"How long would all that take?"

"Months, if we're lucky. Years, more likely," said Dr. Blackwater.

Chip felt his heart sink. They didn't have months or years. At the rate construction was proceeding, the jut would be leveled and poured with concrete within weeks.

"There might be another way," Mary Tiger said quietly. "A way that doesn't depend on the white man's courts."

"What do you mean?" Chip asked.

The elderly woman looked at Joseph Osceola, who nodded slowly. "There are old ways of protecting sacred land, ways that call upon the spirits themselves to defend what is theirs."

"I don't understand," Chip said, though he was

starting to wonder if the pelican incident was more than coincidence.

"A ceremony," Dr. Blackwater explained. "A ritual calling upon the ancestors to protect their resting place. It's not something the tribe does lightly, and it's not something that can be undone once it's begun."

"Would it work?" Tanner asked.

Joseph Osceola's weathered face was grave, though his eyes twinkled with mischief. "The spirits of our ancestors are powerful, but they are also unpredictable. Once awakened, they will seek justice in their own way, in their own time. Those who have harmed the sacred land will face consequences, but so might anyone connected to the desecration."

"Including us?" Jake asked.

"Including your family," Mary Tiger said, looking directly at Chip. "The spirits do not distinguish between those who order the destruction and those who profit from it. If your uncle's company has disturbed our ancestors, the curse will fall on all who bear the Waverly name."

Chip then asked, "What kind of consequences?"

"Misfortune. Illness. Financial ruin. Sometimes death," Joseph Osceola's voice was matter-of-fact, as if he were discussing the weather. "The spirits are patient, but they are thorough."

"There has to be another way," Chip said. "Some

way to stop the construction without putting my family at risk."

"Perhaps," Dr. Blackwater said, "but it would require your uncle to voluntarily halt construction and restore the land to its natural state. And it would require him to acknowledge the sacred nature of the site, and ask forgiveness from the tribal elders."

"Fat chance of that happening," Jake muttered, then immediately looked embarrassed. "Sorry, I mean slim probability of that occurring."

"Then you must choose," Joseph Osceola said firmly. "Allow the desecration to continue, or accept the consequences of calling upon our ancestors for justice."

The room fell silent except for the distant sound of drums from somewhere deeper in the cultural center. Chip stared at the artifacts in Joseph Osceola's weathered hands, feeling the weight of generations pressing down on him. The carved bone ornaments seemed to pulse with their own inner light in the lamplight, and for a moment he could almost hear whispers in a language he didn't understand.

"How long do I have to decide?" he asked finally.

"The ceremony must be performed during the new moon," Mary Tiger said, consulting what appeared to be both a traditional calendar and her iPhone. "That gives you three days."

"And if I choose not to go through with it?"

"Then the sacred island dies, and with it, the resting place of our ancestors," Joseph Osceola said simply. "And the spirits will remember who allowed it to happen. Plus, the pelicans are just getting started."

Dr. Blackwater walked them to their car after the meeting, her expression troubled. "Chip, I need you to understand something. The elders weren't speaking metaphorically in there. They truly believe that disturbing that burial ground will bring supernatural consequences to your family."

"Do you believe it?" Chip asked.

She was quiet for a long moment, looking out across the dark expanse of the Everglades. "I'm a scientist. I believe in data and evidence and peer review. But I'm also Miccosukee, and I've seen things that science can't explain. What I can tell you is that every single attempt to develop that land over the past century has ended in disaster for the developers."

"Tanner mentioned that earlier. The bankruptcies, the accidents, the sinkhole."

"My grandmother kept records of all of it. She said the spirits were protecting the sacred land the only way they could. When it comes to your uncle, they won't just target the construction company or the investors. If the ceremony is performed, the curse will follow bloodlines."

Chip felt his stomach drop. "My parents. My sisters. Jake and Tanner's parents as well."

"Everyone who shares Waverly blood, and everyone who profits from Waverly money."

The drive back to Hillsboro Mile was filled with nervous laughter as they recounted the pelican incident, each of the cousins trying to lighten the mood. When they reached the point where their routes diverged, Jake finally spoke.

"You're not seriously considering this, are you? Some kind of ancient curse? I mean, come on, a pelican landing on a bulldozer isn't exactly supernatural warfare."

"I don't know what I'm considering," Chip said, "but I know I can't let that sanctuary be destroyed."

"Then we find another way," Tanner said, grinning. "We go to the media, we contact environmental groups, we chain ourselves to the bulldozers if we have to. Maybe we can train that pelican to be our mascot."

"And if none of that works?"

"Then we acknowledge that we made an effort," Jake stated. "However, we won't jeopardize our entire family over some supernatural nonsense."

After his cousins got out and left in their own car, Chip sat in his car for a long time, staring at an amber "turtle safe" street lamp. His phone buzzed with a family group text from his father: "Working late again. Don't wait up. Love you."

On impulse, he drove to his uncle's office instead

of going home. The Waverly Construction offices were in a converted architecture building with wood and coral panels off A1A in nearby Deerfield Beach, and Chip knew his uncle often worked late into the evening. The parking lot was nearly empty except for Marcus's BMW, and a company truck that had what looked suspiciously like pelican droppings on its windshield.

The front door was locked, but Chip had the security code memorized. The offices were dim, illuminated only by a light in his uncle's corner office.

"Uncle Marcus?" he called out as he approached the door.

His uncle looked up from a pile of blueprints spread across his desk, his face showing surprise and then something that might have been guilt. A half-eaten sub from Whale's Rib sat close to the blueprints, and what looked like environmental impact charts.

"Chip! What are you doing here so late?"

"I wanted to talk to you about the Wahoo Bay project."

Marcus Waverly was a larger, more windblown version of Chip's father, despite being the younger of the two, with the same dark hair now streaked with gray and the same intense eyes. But where Liam dealt in abstract financial concepts, Marcus had spent decades working with concrete and steel, and it showed in his calloused hands and sun-weathered face.

"What about it?" Marcus asked, but his tone was guarded as he tried to casually slide his sandwich away from the blueprints.

"I know about the pelican sanctuary. I know about the Miccosukee burial ground. I know you've been systematically destroying the ecosystem for months to make the environmental impact look less severe."

His uncle's face went through several expressions, surprise, anger, and frustration. For a split second, he almost defaults to denial, but ultimately simply says, "How did you find out?"

"Does it matter? The question is, are you going to stop the construction?"

Marcus leaned back in his chair, suddenly looking older than his fifty-two years.

"Chip, you don't understand the complexities involved here. This isn't just about building condos."

"Then explain it to me."

His uncle was quiet for a long moment, staring at the blueprints on his desk. "Your father and I, we're in trouble. Serious financial trouble. The market crash in 2020 wiped out most of our liquid assets, and we've got creditors breathing down our necks. He probably didn't tell you that he invested the last of his liquidity into my current construction portfolio, and Wahoo Bay Island is the centerpiece to turn it all around."

"No…I had no idea…but that still doesn't explain why you decided to destroy a sacred burial ground?"

"I decided to save our family from bankruptcy!" Marcus's voice rose, then he caught himself and lowered it again. "The Pelican Pointe development isn't just another project, Chip. It's our lifeline. The pre-sales alone will generate enough cash flow to keep both our companies afloat."

"What about the environmental protections? The sacred land designation? And the curse everyone used to talk about?"

Marcus gestured with his hand. "Environmental protections can be challenged in court. Sacred land designations can be quietly removed if you know the right people and have enough money to make it worth their while. And the curse is just another fish tale. Enough."

"You bribed officials?"

"I made campaign contributions to politicians who understand the importance of economic development. There's a difference."

"Not to the pelicans. Not to the Miccosukee ancestors buried on that island."

Marcus stood up, his face flushing with anger. "Don't lecture me about responsibility, Chip. Everything your family has, your house, your education, your trust fund, it all comes from Waverly money. That money from the old Flagler railroad days ran out a long time ago. They said it never would, but it did. And now that money comes from development projects just like this one."

"Not like this one. This one is different."

"How? Because you've suddenly developed a conscience about environmental issues and your new buzz word is 'Blue Economy?' Because you've been talking to some Native American activists who want to turn every piece of undeveloped land into a shrine?" Marcus rubbed his forehead dramatically.

"Because it's wrong," Chip said simply. "And because if you don't stop it, something terrible is going to happen to our family."

Marcus stared at his nephew, seeing something in his expression that made him pause. "What are you talking about? And please tell me this isn't about that pelican run-in yesterday."

Chip told him about the meeting with the tribal elders, about the curse, about the ceremony that would be performed in three days if the construction didn't stop. His uncle listened without interruption, his face growing increasingly skeptical.

"You're talking about superstition, Chip. Ancient myths and folklore. Next you'll be telling me that pelican was sent by the spirits."

"What about all the other developers who tried to build on that land? The bankruptcies, the accidents, the mysterious disasters?"

"Coincidences. Bad luck. Poor planning."

"Or maybe the spirits of the Miccosukee ancestors really are protecting their burial ground. Maybe they're recruiting local wildlife."

Marcus shook his head, chuckling despite himself. "I can't believe I'm having this conversation with a member of my own family. You're talking about throwing away millions of dollars and destroying two family businesses because of some ghost stories and a pelican."

"I'm talking about doing the right thing before it's too late."

"It's already too late," Marcus said quietly. "Even if I wanted to stop the project, which I don't, I can't. We've got investors, contractors, pre-sale agreements. The legal and financial consequences of backing out now would destroy us just as surely as bankruptcy."

"Then we'll find another way to solve the financial problems. Maybe there's money in selling the railroad coupler patent, I don't know, but it's worth checking."

"With what? Your father's hedge fund is hemorrhaging money, and my construction company is leveraged to the hilt. This development is our only chance. Though I admit selling that railroad patent isn't the worst idea you've had."

Chip stared at his uncle, seeing the desperation behind the humor. "What if I could prove that the permits were obtained illegally? That the environmental impact assessments were falsified?"

"You can't prove that because it's not true."

"Isn't it? You just admitted that you've been systematically destroying the ecosystem for months. You admitted that you made payments to have the sacred land designation removed."

Marcus's face went pale. "Those weren't illegal payments. They were legitimate campaign contributions."

"To officials who then removed environmental protections from land that had been protected for decades? A federal prosecutor might see it differently."

"Are you threatening me?" Marcus asked, nervously adjusting his watch.

"I'm trying to save you. Save all of us. If you don't stop this project voluntarily, I'm going to do everything in my power to stop it legally. And if that doesn't work…"

"If that doesn't work, what? You'll let some tribal elders cast a spell on my bulldozers?" Marcus scoffed, frantically pacing the room.

Marcus stared at his nephew for a long moment, then sank back into his chair. "You really believe this curse nonsense, don't you?"

"I believe that some things are bigger than money," Chip said. "And I believe that actions have consequences."

Chapter 4: Part Two "Really Weird"

His uncle's phone rang, the shrill sound cutting through the tension in the room. Marcus glanced at the caller ID and frowned, fumbling with the phone and nearly dropping it. "It's my site foreman at the Coral Gables project. I need to take this."

"Marcus here," he said, putting the phone on speaker. "What's the emergency, Rodriguez?"

"Boss, we've got a serious problem. The crane collapsed about an hour ago. Nobody was here this late, so no one was hurt, but it took out half the scaffolding and damaged the foundation work we just finished. Oh, and flocks of pelicans just showed up out of nowhere and are sitting on the equipment under the work lights. Really weird."

Marcus blinked. "What do you mean it collapsed? That crane was inspected last week. Wait, did you say pelicans?"

"That's the weird part about the crane. The inspection records show everything was perfect, but when the investigators got here, they found stress fractures in the main support beam that look like they've been developing for months. As for the pelicans, yeah, they're still here. Just sitting on the crane wreckage like they own the place."

"That's impossible. That crane is only two years old."

"I know, boss. But there's more. The concrete we poured yesterday? It's cracking. All of it. The lab says the mix was wrong, but I was there when we tested it. Everything was perfect."

Chip watched his uncle's face as the implications sank in. The Coral Gables project was Waverly Construction's second-largest job, a luxury hotel that was supposed to be completed by Christmas.

"How much are we looking at in damages?" Marcus asked quietly, his voice cracking slightly.

"Minimum two million, probably closer to three. And that's if we can get back on schedule within a month."

After hanging up, Marcus sat in silence, staring at the blueprints scattered across his desk. "It's just bad luck," he said in an unconvincing tone, with his hands visibly shaking.

Chip's phone vibrated with a message from Jake: "There's an emergency at the marina. Dad's boat engine blew up. Thankfully, no one was injured, but the boat is destroyed. The insurance company suspects sabotage, but the security cameras captured nothing. Also, a pelican was sitting right in front of the security camera, just observing. It was as if he knew something."

Another text followed immediately from Tanner:

"Weird accident at Mom's bakery. All the freezers failed simultaneously tonight AND a family of raccoons somehow got into the kitchen! Repair guys say they've never seen anything like it."

Chip showed the messages to his uncle, whose face grew increasingly pale. "This is just coincidence," Marcus said, but his hands were shaking as he reached for his phone.

He dialed a number and waited. "Peterson? It's Marcus Waverly. I need you to check on all our active job sites. Right now! I don't care what time it is…just do it and call me back. And if you see any unusual animal activity, document it."

Within twenty minutes, Marcus's phone had rung four more times. Equipment failures at the Fort Lauderdale shopping center, plus all the porta-potties had inexplicably tipped over in perfect domino formation. Mysterious foundation problems at the Boca Raton office complex, where workers reported their hard hats kept flying off in windless conditions. A sinkhole that had opened overnight at the Delray Beach residential project, swallowing two bulldozers, and somehow a food truck had appeared selling "Pete the Pelican's Prime Time Tacos" to the bewildered construction crew.

"This isn't possible," Marcus whispered, staring at the growing list of disasters. "Equipment doesn't just fail simultaneously across multiple sites."

"Unless something is making it fail," Chip said quietly.

His uncle looked up at him with eyes that now held a flicker of fear. "You think this is connected to, to what you told me about the ceremony? The spirits have a sense of humor? What?!?"

"The tribal elders said the spirits are patient but thorough. Maybe they're sending a warning. A really creative one."

Marcus's phone rang again. This time it was Chip's father, Liam.

"Marcus, what the hell is going on? I just got calls from three of our major investors. They're hearing rumors about problems with Waverly Construction projects. Also, someone tonight posted a TikTok of our bulldozers in that sinkhole set to circus music. It has two million views already. Our stock price is already down twelve percent in after-hours trading."

"Liam, I…"

Chip watched his uncle's face crumble as the full scope of the disaster became clear. The curse wasn't just targeting construction equipment and buildings. It was systematically destroying everything the Waverly family had built over decades.

"The ceremony hasn't even been performed yet," Chip said softly. "This is just the beginning. Wait until you see what they do with the company picnic."

Marcus looked at him with desperate eyes. "What

do I have to do to make it stop? And can we please do something about these pelicans?"

Marcus was quiet for a long moment, then reached for his phone again. "I'm calling McCarther. If we're going to stop this, we need to understand our legal options."

Kenny McCarther had been the Waverly family attorney for over thirty years, a sharp-eyed man in his seventies who had handled everything from the handed down Flagler Railroad patents, to Marcus's first construction contracts, and to Chip's parents' prenuptial agreement. His office was in a downtown Fort Lauderdale high-rise, but he answered his personal cell phone on the second ring despite the late hour.

"Marcus? What's wrong? You sound terrible."

"Ken, I need you to pull the original deed for the Wahoo Bay property. The one from 1923."

"At this hour? Marcus, whatever's going on can wait until morning."

"No, it can't. I need that deed now. And I need you to look for any restrictions or covenants that might affect development rights."

There was a pause on the other end of the line. "Marcus, I've reviewed that deed a dozen times over the past year. There are no development restrictions beyond the standard environmental protections."

"Look again. Please. Check the archives, check the original filing, check everything."

McCarther sighed. "Fine. I'll drive to the office and pull the files, but this better be important."

While they waited, Marcus paced his office like a caged animal, occasionally glancing at his phone as if expecting more bad news. Chip sat quietly, thinking about everything the tribal elders had told him about the sacred nature of the land.

At this time of night, the county records office was of course closed. However, McCarther has always made it his business to know all the right people, namely the security guards, to let him in after hours. Amazing what a few palmed 20's can do.

An hour later, McCarther called back, his voice strained. "Marcus, we have a problem. A big problem."

"What kind of problem?" Marcus said, even though he knew what the problem was already.

"I found the original deed from 1923. The one in our files is a copy, and apparently not a complete one. The original has an additional page that was never included in our records."

Marcus put the phone on speaker. "That happens all the time, no need to worry about one page," Marcus coyly tried to change the subject.

"There's a covenant that requires written approval from the Miccosukee Tribal Council for any development or alteration of the land. The covenant was signed by the original purchaser, James Deering, and witnessed by both a federal judge and a tribal representative."

Marcus didn't say anything, but he was already very familiar with James Deering, who was the famed builder of the Vizcaya Estate (now museum) in Miami.

Chip felt his heart racing and chimed in. "Is the covenant still legally binding?"

"Absolutely. Covenants like this run with the land in perpetuity. Every subsequent owner is bound by the terms, whether they know about it or not."

"How is it possible that we didn't know about this?" Marcus demanded, his frustration mounting, not wanting Chip to hear the truth that incoming.

McCarther's voice was grim. "You did and you know it! You deliberately removed that page from the deed copies in our files. You asked me for a chance to go over the files in private. The original is still on file with the county clerk, but it's been misfiled under the wrong property number. If I hadn't specifically searched for the 1923 filing date, I never would have found it. Anyone who's worked on the Wahoo Bay project over the past year: the title company, the environmental consultants, the permitting attorneys, everything was based on missing information, files you took, Marcus."

Marcus's face was pale. "Ken, if this covenant is

valid, what does it mean for the development?" not admitting any guilt.

Despite McCarther's indignation, like any good attorney, he knows that a client's bad decisions usually just lead to more work for him anyways. About that time, his demeanor changed back to his standard professional tone, ready to give his sound legal advice to a client in trouble.

"It means every permit you've obtained is invalid. Every contract you've signed is void. And if you've already begun construction without tribal approval, you're in violation of federal law."

The room fell silent except for the hum of the air conditioning. Chip could see his uncle processing the implications, not just the financial disaster, but the potential criminal liability.

"There's more," McCarther continued. "I did some digging into the permitting process. Several of the officials who approved your applications have received significant campaign contributions from shell companies connected to Waverly Construction. The timing of the contributions and the permit approvals is, to say the least, problematic."

"Problematic how?"

"The kind of problematic that attracts federal prosecutors. Marcus, you need to shut down that construction site immediately and get yourself a criminal defense attorney."

After hanging up, Marcus slumped in his chair, looking defeated. "Thirty years of building this company, and it's all going to disappear because of one piece of paper."

"It doesn't have to," Chip said. "You heard what Dr. Blackwater said. If you voluntarily halt construction and ask the tribal elders for forgiveness, there might be a way to resolve this."

"You mean grovel to a bunch of, well, you know" Marcus caught himself before finishing the sentence. "I'm sorry. I didn't mean that."

"Yes, you did. And that is why you got rid of the piece of paper in the first place. Retribution is coming for you unless you change your ways right now."

5

THE PROBLEM WITH PELICANS

Later that week, with the deadline looming, news came in that would have been hilarious if it weren't so financially devastating. Chip's phone buzzed at 6 AM with a text from Jake: "Turn on Channel 7 News. NOW."

The local morning show was running a segment called "Pelican Pandemonium: Birds Gone Wild at South Florida Construction Sites." The reporter, a perky blonde woman named Jessica Braley, stood in front of what used to be the Coral Gables crane, now decorated with an impressive collection of pelican nests.

"What started as isolated incidents of aggressive bird behavior has escalated into what some are calling an organized avian uprising," Jessica reported with all seriousness. "Witnesses report pelicans working in coordinated groups to sabotage construction equipment, steal workers' lunches, and even make nests in the driver seats of the cranes."

The camera panned to show Jerry Rodriguez, the construction foreman, looking haggard. "It's like they're planning this stuff," he said, glancing nervously at the sky. "Yesterday, three pelicans dive-bombed me simultaneously. That's not natural behavior. That's military precision."

"Have you considered that maybe the pelicans want their homes back?" Jessica asked.

"Lady, I've been working construction for twenty years. I know the difference between birds and birds with a vendetta. These pelicans have it out for Waverly Construction specifically. They ignore all the other sites. It's like they've got our company logo memorized."

The segment continued with footage of pelicans systematically removing hard hats from workers' heads, untying safety ropes, and in one particularly impressive display, using their beaks to turn off bulldozer engines. The piece concluded with a bird expert from the Tropical Audubon Society explaining that such coordinated behavior was "unprecedented in pelican research, and frankly, a little unsettling."

Chip's phone rang immediately after the segment ended. It was his father, and he sounded panicked.

"Chip, have you seen the news? Our company is being portrayed as the target of some kind of bird conspiracy. The phones haven't stopped ringing. Half the calls are from reporters wanting to interview us about 'The Pelican Wars,' and the other half are from investors demanding to know why our stock price has dropped thirty percent overnight."

"Dad, where are you?"

"At your uncle's office, trying to do damage control, but it's not working. Someone posted the video footage of our bulldozers in that sinkhole again as a remix on YouTube set to the theme from 'Jaws.' It has fifty million views."

"What about Uncle Marcus?"

"He's barricaded himself in his office. Won't answer his phone, won't see anyone. The only communication we've had is a note he slipped under the door that says, 'The pelicans know.' What does that even mean?"

"Um, not sure," he said, trying to shield his father from the full story. "I'll be right over."

Chip found his uncle exactly where his father had

described, locked in his office, surrounded by empty coffee cups.

"Uncle Marcus? It's me, Chip."

The door opened a crack, revealing one bloodshot eye. "Are you alone? No birds?"

"No birds. Can I come in?"

Marcus opened the door just wide enough for Chip to slip through, then immediately locked it behind him. The office looked like a war room, with charts and maps covering every surface, red string connecting various photographs of pelicans, and a whiteboard covered with what looked like flight patterns.

"I've been studying them," Marcus said, gesturing wildly at his makeshift command center. "They're not random. They're organized. Look at this."

He pointed to a map of South Florida with red pins marking every Waverly Construction site. "Every single project has been hit. But it's not just equipment failures anymore. It's psychological warfare now."

"What do you mean?"

"Yesterday, a pelican somehow got into the Port St. Lucie site office and rearranged all the blueprints into the word 'NO.' The workers were so freaked out they refused to come back. And this morning, the entire flock at the Wahoo Bay Island site was spotted flying in a formation that spelled out 'STOP' in the sky. Jerry got it on video."

Chip looked at the whiteboard more closely, and could see his uncle was right. The pelican attacks did seem to follow a pattern, hitting Waverly projects with surgical precision, while leaving competitors' sites completely untouched.

"Uncle Marcus, you need to listen to me. This isn't just about angry birds. The tribal elders are performing the ceremony tonight."

Marcus spun around. "Tonight? But you said we had three days!"

"That was three days ago. You've been holed up in here for seventy-two hours surviving on turkey subs, coffee, and conspiracy theories, ever since our call with McCarther."

The color drained from his uncle's face. "What happens during the ceremony?"

"I don't know exactly. But Dr. Blackwater said once it begins, it can't be stopped. The curse will follow bloodlines until either the sacred land is restored or..." Chip trailed off.

"Or what?"

"Or until the Waverly family line ends."

Marcus stared at him for a long moment, then walked to his window and looked out at the construction site across the street. A lone pelican sat on the roof of the building, seemingly watching the office. When it saw Marcus, it spread its wings in what looked disturbingly like that demon on top of the mountain in that old Disney movie.

"That's the same pelican that's been there for three days," Marcus whispered. "I've named him 'Genghis Pelikhan.' I think he's their leader."

"Uncle Marcus, you're starting to sound a little…"

"Crazy? Maybe. But crazy people don't usually have their entire life's work systematically destroyed by coordinated bird attacks. I even saw a Cormorant and a Snowy Egret sitting with the pelicans today. I think they're recruiting mercenaries outside of their species!" He turned back to Chip. "So, what do you want me to do? What can I do?"

"Come with me to the ceremony. Ask the elders for forgiveness. Agree to restore the land."

"And if I don't?"

"We'll all find out, won't we?" Chip said.

6

THE TRIAL OF THE PELICANS

By the time Chip and Marcus arrived on the island at the Wahoo Bay construction site, a crowd had already gathered.

What they saw was a stunning sight that Chip had never seen before. Hundreds of magnificent pelicans had gathered on the island. They were clustered closely together, their long bills resting against their chests, forming a unified mass. A coalition, perhaps. An impenetrable barrier for anyone trying to get through.

"This is impossible," Marcus breathed, staring at the avian assembly.

"Maybe these aren't just ordinary birds," Chip suggested.

Dr. Blackwater appeared at Chip's elbow, having somehow materialized from the crowd without him noticing. "The ceremony begins at sunset," she said quietly. "But it looks like the spirits have already started their own proceedings."

"What are they doing?"

"If I had to guess? The pelicans are serving as proxies for the ancestral spirits, weighing the evidence of desecration against the possibility of redemption."

As if responding to her words, the large brown pelican let out a long, mournful cry that was immediately echoed by the entire assembly. The sound sent chills down Chip's spine, and caused several people in the crowd to step back nervously.

"How will they decide?" Marcus asked, his voice barely above a whisper.

"That depends on what you're willing to do right now," Dr. Blackwater replied. "The spirits are giving you one final chance to make this right."

Marcus stepped forward, his legs shaking slightly as he approached the giant gathering of pelicans.

"I," Marcus began, then stopped, overwhelmed by the surreal nature of addressing a pod of pelicans. "I don't know what to say."

"Start with the truth," Dr. Blackwater suggested. "Tell them why you're here."

Marcus took a deep breath. "I came here to build condominiums. To make money. I knew this land was protected, and I found ways around those protections, because I thought profit was more important than preservation." His voice grew stronger as he continued. "I was wrong. I've spent the last three days watching everything I've built over thirty years crumble, and I finally understand that some things are more valuable than money."

"I want to make this right," Marcus continued. "I want to restore this land to its natural state and ensure it's protected forever. But I don't know how to undo what I've already done."

A massive pelican let out another cry, this one somehow different, less mournful, more questioning. The sound rippled through the assembly, and Chip noticed that several of the birds were now looking directly at him.

"I think they want to hear from you too," Dr. Blackwater said.

Chip stepped forward, feeling the weight of hundreds of avian eyes upon him. "My name is Chip Waverly. This is my family's company, which means this is my responsibility too. I wish I would have known sooner, and I could have protected this place before any damage was done."

He paused, looking out over the sacred island where bulldozers sat silent among the pines. "But I'm here now, and I'm asking for your help. Help us understand what we need to do to heal this land." The large pelican spread his wings wide, and suddenly the entire assembly took flight. They circled the construction site three times, their formation creating intricate patterns against the darkening sky.

"What does that mean?" Marcus asked.

Dr. Blackwater smiled for the first time since Chip had met her. "I think it means they're willing to work with you, but the real ceremony still needs to happen. The tribal elders are waiting."

7

THE CEREMONY OF RESTORATION

The Miccosukee ceremony took place at the very center of the devastation caused by the now halted construction on Wahoo Bay Island. As the sun set, painting the Hillsboro Lighthouse in shades of gold and crimson, Chip found himself standing in a circle with his uncle, Jake and Tanner, the tribal elders, and Dr. Blackwater.

Joseph Osceola had traded his casual clothes for traditional ceremonial dress, a colorful patchwork shirt and a headdress adorned with feathers and beads. Mary Tiger wore a long skirt decorated with intricate beadwork that seemed to shimmer in the firelight. The transformation was striking; they were no longer just the humble, soft-spoken people he met at the cultural center, but powerful spiritual leaders carrying the weight of centuries.

"The ceremony of restoration is not just about healing the land," Joseph Osceola explained, his voice carrying easily across the water. "It's about healing the relationship between the living and the dead, between the present and the past, between those who take and those who give."

A fire had been built in the center of the circle, and the elders began to chant in the Miccosukee language. The words were foreign to Chip, but their meaning seemed to resonate in his bones. The chanting grew louder, more complex, with multiple voices weaving together in harmonies that seemed to make the very air vibrate.

Mary Tiger stepped forward, carrying a bowl filled with what looked like herbs and salt water from Wahoo Bay. "Marcus Waverly," she said, her voice formal and commanding. "Do you acknowledge the harm you have caused to this sacred land?"

"I do," Marcus replied, his voice steady despite the tremor in his hands.

"Do you pledge to restore what has been damaged and to protect what remains?"

"I do," Marcus said, and this time his voice carried conviction that surprised even Chip.

"Then, drink from the bowl of reconciliation, and let the spirits judge your sincerity."

Marcus accepted the bowl with both hands and drank deeply. The liquid was bitter, salty, and earthy, with an aftertaste that seemed to linger not just on his tongue but in his very soul. As he lowered the bowl, a warm breeze swept across the island, carrying with it the sound of wings.

The pelicans had returned.

They came not as the organized army that had terrorized construction sites, but as individual birds, landing quietly around the perimeter of the ceremony.

"The spirits accept your offering," Mary Tiger announced, and Chip could swear he heard approval in the gentle calls of the pelicans. "But words alone cannot heal what has been broken. The restoration must be complete, not just of the land, but of the trust that has been violated."

Joseph Osceola stepped forward, carrying what appeared to be an ancient document wrapped in deerskin. "This is the original covenant, signed by James Deering in 1923. He aligned himself with the Miccosukee tribe, with intentions to build another tropical escape that existed in harmony with our sacred land, but he passed in 1925 before the drawings were ever finalized for tribal approval. Without any direct descendants to inherit the land, so began the uncertain future of Wahoo Bay Island. Now tonight, over 100 years after this document was signed, we renew it."

He unrolled the document, revealing not just the legal language McCarther had described, but intricate drawings that seemed to map out the entire ecosystem of Wahoo Bay, every pine, every nesting ground, every sacred site.

"There's more," Mary Tiger said. "When we retrieved this document from our archives, there was a photo from the date it was signed. We thought you might be interested to see it."

Marcus studied the photo from left to right. He saw a few tribal elders, a man he presumed to be James Deering signing the document, but slowly his eyes widened as he panned to the right edge of the photo.

"Thomas Waverly," he whispered, recognizing his great-grandfather from an old photo kept on the family mantle since he was a child. "I never knew he had any connection to the tribe."

"Your great-grandfather, Thomas, who not only invented the railroad coupler that made train track building secure for travel, but made it safer for those who would be installing it. He understood what you forgot," Mary Tiger said. "That some places are not meant to be owned, only protected. He served as witness to the signing of this covenant, since the word of a Miccosukee tribe member did not hold the weight of a white man's testimony in court at the time. He recognized the covenant not as a burden, but as a privilege."

"I never knew," Marcus admitted. "My father never spoke of any covenant, any responsibility to the tribe. I grew up thinking this was just another piece of property."

"Then tonight, we restore not just the land, but the memory," Mary Tiger declared.

"And we expand the circle of guardianship."

She turned to Chip. "You spoke truth to the pelicans. You chose conscience over profit. Will you accept the role of guardian of this land?"

Chip felt the weight of the moment, the eyes of ancestors both living and dead upon him. But alongside the gravity came something unexpected, joy. For the first time in months, he knew exactly what he was supposed to do.

"I will," he said, and meant it completely. Jake and Tanner were standing by his side.

The ceremony continued deep into the night, with chanting, storytelling, and the gradual revelation of a plan that was both ambitious and beautiful. The Wahoo Bay site would be transformed into something unprecedented, a joint venture between the Waverly family and the Miccosukee tribe that would serve as a nature preserve, marine biology lab and a cultural center.

Even the idea of a blue economy structure for this place was being considered, meaning the sustainable use of ocean resources for economic growth, improved livelihoods, and job creation, while also preserving the health of marine ecosystems. It would encompass a wide range of economic activities related to oceans, seas, and coasts, including both traditional sectors like fisheries and shipping, and emerging areas like marine renewable energy and biotechnology.

"Think of it as the opposite of development," Dr. Blackwater explained as they sat around the dying fire. "Instead of imposing human structures on the natural world, we'll create spaces where people can experience the ecosystem as it was meant to be."

The financial details of the venture were surprisingly encouraging. The federal government offered substantial grants for environmental restoration projects, especially those involving tribal partnerships. Several environmental organizations had already expressed interest in funding the initiative. And the pelicans, as if sensing the change in direction, had begun to disperse peacefully back to their natural roosting sites.

"What about the investors?" Marcus asked. "The people who put money into Pelican Pointe expecting luxury condos?"

Suddenly, Liam Waverly's voice answered from amongst the crowd. "We, as a family, decide to make a sacrifice for once! We will sell the patent for the train track coupler to Amtrak. That will bring in millions and get the investors repaid!" Liam made his way up to stand beside Marcus, who was unaware Liam had been watching the proceedings. When he was close enough, Liam put his hand on his brother's shoulder in the kind of reassuring manner that could only come from an older brother. "I already spoke to McCarther. He's apparently been in contact with Amtrak through his government connections for years, just waiting until we were ready to let go of it."

Joseph Osceola smiled. "The spirits work in mysterious ways. Sometimes what looks like destruction is actually preparation for something greater."

As dawn broke over Hillsboro Inlet, painting the sky in soft pastels, Chip felt a sense of completion he'd never experienced. All three young men had pulled off the impossible.

8

THE PELICAN POINTE PIVOT

Three weeks after the ceremony, Chip stood in a tiki-roofed, round building, which now was the headquarters of the Wahoo Bay Restoration Project. The walls didn't display glossy renderings of luxury condominiums, but showcased detailed ecological surveys, architectural plans for elevated boardwalks, and a large map marking every sacred site on the island. It also contained preliminary drawings for the marine habitat restoration. The Waverly family worked tirelessly to implement creative environmental solutions for Wahoo Bay

Island, drawing inspiration from the founders and innovators at Ocean Rescue Alliance International, while also creating some of their own restoration strategies based upon the unique ecology of the area. Blue, Conservation-Based, Development Economy would be the new goal.

His father sat across from him, reviewing financial projections with the kind of intense focus he usually reserved for hedge fund portfolios. The numbers were coming together amazingly well: federal restoration grants, state environmental incentives, and private donations from conservation groups had already covered sixty percent of the project's initial costs.

"I have to admit," Liam said, setting down his calculator, "selling the patent was the most resourceful way to pay back the investors and work towards the future."

"More sustainable in every sense," Chip agreed, watching through the window as a team of marine biologists, including his sister Sloan, worked alongside Miccosukee tribal members to catalog the mangrove ecosystem.

Marcus entered the office carrying a stack of permits, Jake and Tanner in tow. His demeanor completely transformed from the paranoid, self-serving, devious man he'd been just weeks before. "The Army Corps of Engineers approved our wetland restoration plan," he announced, grinning broadly.

"And the county is fast-tracking our permits for the visitor center."

"Any pelican interference?" Chip asked with a smile.

"None whatsoever, only the occasional fly-by to catch a fish or two," Marcus said with a light-hearted laugh not heard from him in months. "And since the pelicans stopped their coordinated attacks, it looks like we can get back to work at our other construction sites as well. The damages at our Coral Gables project were not as catastrophic as we thought. Insurance will cover the cost of the collapsed crane, and we took out a small bridge loan to complete the condos. Once those sell, we can use those funds to complete our other working projects, and we should be in profit within 18 months across the board!" Marcus high-fived everyone around the room like he was in the starting lineup for the Miami Heat.

The transformation of Marcus had been perhaps the most remarkable aspect of the entire project. The man who had once viewed environmental regulations as obstacles to profit, now spoke passionately about habitat restoration and sustainable development. He'd even enrolled in a University of Florida extension course on wetland ecology. His sons are thinking about that class as well, but this really interested Chip most of all.

"Speaking of construction," Marcus continued,

"we need to make a decision about the existing foundation work on the land. The engineers say we can either remove it completely or incorporate it into the visitor center design."

Dr. Blackwater looked up from the species inventory she'd been reviewing. "What do the tribal elders prefer?"

"That's the interesting part," Marcus said. "Joseph Osceola suggested we leave some of it as a reminder. He called it 'scar tissue that tells a story.' We could build interpretive displays around the old foundation, showing what almost happened and why preservation matters."

Chip nodded thoughtfully. "A cautionary tale built right into the landscape. I like it."

The phone rang, and Chip answered to find Jessica Braley from WSVN Channel 7 on the line. The reporter who had once covered "The Pelican Wars" had become an unexpected ally, documenting the restoration project with the same enthusiasm she'd once brought to bird-related chaos.

"Chip, I've got great news," Jessica said, her voice bubbling with excitement. "The Nature Conservancy wants to feature Wahoo Bay in their national magazine. They're calling it a model for how private development can pivot to conservation without financial ruin. That's what makes what you do unique."

"That's fantastic. When do they want to visit?"

"Next week. And they want to interview the whole family, plus the tribal elders."

After hanging up, Chip shook his head in amazement. "I never thought I'd live to see the day when our family business would be famous for not building something." Jake and Tanner agreed.

"The best part," his father added, "is that our stock price has actually recovered. Investors are calling it the 'Waverly Pivot,' and environmental funds are buying in because we've proven that conservation can be profitable."

9

THE UNEXPECTED ALLY

Months later brought a visitor none of them had expected. Chip, Jake, and Tanner were reviewing drawings that would help them build nest stands over the summer. Then, someone named Patricia Hensworth showed up on the scene. The name was familiar, but it took them a moment to place it. She was the lead investor in the original Pelican Pointe development, the woman who had put up nine million dollars expecting luxury waterfront condos.

Patricia Hensworth was a petite woman in her sixties with silver hair and kind eyes, wearing practical hiking boots and carrying what appeared to be a well-used field guide to Florida birds.

"Hello boys!" she said exuberantly. "I believe we need to talk."

Chip pulled over an empty rattan chair for her to sit on, unclear of where this was heading.

"I'm here because I think you've done something remarkable, and I want to be part of it," she continued.

"I'm sorry, what?" Chip replied, somewhat taken by surprise.

Patricia smiled, pulling out a tablet and swiping to a series of photographs. "These are from my visit to the site yesterday. I hope you don't mind that I took the liberty of exploring the area with one of your marine biologists."

The photos showed the restored mangrove areas, the carefully planned boardwalk routes, and several shots of the visitor center construction. But what caught Chip's attention were the final images: Patricia herself, standing knee-deep in brackish water, helping to plant new mangrove seedlings while a brown pelican watched approvingly from a nearby branch.

"Ms. Hensworth, I have to ask, aren't you upset about not building luxury condos? You got your money back, but nothing more."

"Upset? Chip, I've been waiting forty years for someone to do exactly what you boys are doing."

She leaned forward, her eyes bright with enthusiasm. "I didn't invest in Pelican Pointe because I wanted another generic waterfront development. I invested because I hoped someone in your family had inherited your great-great-grandfather's vision."

Chip stared at her. "How do you know about our great-great-grandfather, and what do you mean by 'his vision?'" Jake and Tanner were mesmerized by this.

"Thomas Waverly was my hero. I was fresh out of college, working as a junior researcher for the Florida Audubon Society, when I read about his part of the Flagler railroad. I learned about his love of birds and Florida, but what was most exciting was his history with the Miccosukee tribe, his concerns about progress, and his dream of creating a place where people could experience the magic of Florida without destroying it."

The Waverly boys were speechless, because they never even thought to look up what their great-great-grandfather had done for Florida. His life story was always anchored to the payout portion of this memory, not the human part. "Live and learn," said Chip.

"He believed that private landowners had a responsibility to be stewards, not just developers. When he died, and your great-grandfather took over, that vision died with him."

"So, when you invested in Pelican Pointe?"

"I was gambling that eventually, someone in the Waverly family would remember what Thomas stood for. I've been watching your company for decades, waiting for the right moment. Sometimes, that kind of calling can skip a generation or two…or three in your case," she said with a warm smile. "The wildlife uprising was just the catalyst you needed."

All three boys felt a strange mix of emotions, gratitude, embarrassment, and a deep sense of connection to a family legacy they never knew existed. "What do you want from us now?"

"I want to double my investment, not in condos, but in the restoration project. And I want to establish the Thomas Waverly Foundation for Sustainable Development, with Wahoo Bay Island as our flagship project."

Barely able to contain his excitement, Chip had to call his father into this meeting! Jake and Tanner did the same.

Over the next hour, Patricia outlined a vision to Marcus and Liam that was breathtaking in its scope. The foundation would partner with universities to create a research station on The Mile. They would develop educational programs for schools throughout South Florida. Most importantly, they would serve as a model for other developers facing similar choices between profit and preservation. Bringing to life their promise of a blue economy and all that it entailed.

Together, they created a newly expanded Wahoo Bay Restoration Project, which aimed to protect and restore the ecological integrity of Wahoo Bay, while preserving its cultural significance to the Miccosukee tribe.

Key objectives included:

- *Maintaining the pelican sanctuary and supporting marine wildlife*

- *Operating a world-class environmental research facility*

- *Providing educational programs about ecology and Miccosukee culture*

- *Demonstrating profitable eco-tourism and sustainable development practic*

- *Serving as a model for future conservation-development partnerships*

"The pelicans taught us something important," Patricia said as their meeting concluded. "Sometimes the most powerful force for change isn't human at all. It's the natural world asserting its right to exist."

10

THE WAHOO BAY RESTORATION PROJECT AND RESEARCH STATION

Six months later, the Wahoo Bay Restoration Project and Research Station was officially dedicated in a ceremony that drew environmental scientists, tribal leaders, and curious tourists from across the country. Everyone was amazed how quickly it was built, but it's only natural. With 30 years of experience and the right motivation, Waverly Construction was able to complete it far ahead of schedule. The project is centered at the former Pelican Pointe sales office, transformed into the WBRP headquarters.

The facility includes:

• A state-of-the-art research station built on stilts to minimize environmental impact

• Laboratories and dormitories for visiting researchers

• A visitor center for eco-tourism and educational programs that tell the story of the land's transformation

• Protected pelican nesting areas

• Cultural education facilities operated in partnership with the Miccosukee tribe

The headquarters serves as both an administrative center and a symbol of successful transformation from development to conservation.

For Chip, Jake, and Tanner, the research station represented more than just vindication of their decision to abandon the development project, it became the catalyst for a complete re-imagining of their futures. The constant stream of visiting scientists meant the guys found themselves in conversations about marine biology, water chemistry, and ecosystem dynamics on an almost daily basis. They were also learning about reef habitats, and how to create them. What had once been abstract concepts from high school science classes suddenly became tangible realities they could observe in their own backyard.

Chip was putting together his talking points to reach even more people with this project, "The Wahoo Bay Restoration Project has emerged as a partnership between the Waverly family and the Miccosukee tribe, with support from Patricia Hensworth and the newly established Thomas Waverly Foundation for Sustainable Development. Initial funding came from federal grants, state environmental incentives, and private donations. The project gained recognition for successfully balancing environmental conservation with economic viability."

The research station provided a steady income stream through land lease agreements, guided tour partnerships, and consulting fees for their local expertise. More importantly, it connected them to a network of environmental organizations and grant opportunities the boys never knew existed. Within months, he was fielding calls from universities interested in establishing satellite programs and conservation groups seeking similar restoration projects.

Perhaps most significantly, the station gave

Chip a sense of purpose that none of the other "recommended career paths based upon his aptitudes" could have ever provided. Watching his own sister, Sloan, document the return of species that hadn't been seen in decades, seeing school groups learn about wetland ecology in the visitor center, and knowing that his decision had created something that would benefit the environment for generations, it all felt like the work he was meant to be doing. Even Willow got involved, and her live feed on TikTok garnered millions of views in support of the opening.

The boy who had once felt adrift without purpose was becoming a steward of something more valuable to him and to the world than he had ever imagined.

11

THE CALLING

Three months after the research station's dedication, Chip found himself wading through knee-deep water at 5:30 AM, following Dr. Sarah Lancaster around like some kind of eager puppy. Dr. Lancaster was the station's new marine ecologist, this super smart woman who'd come up from Key Biscayne to run the research programs. What had started as a single visit to check out the research being done on his family's land had somehow turned into this twice-weekly thing that she couldn't seem to quit.

"The salinity levels here are perfect," Dr. Lancaster

announced, holding up a digital probe. "We're seeing juvenile fish populations that haven't been documented in this area for over thirty years."

Chip watched a small school of silver juvenile jacks dart between the mangrove roots, their movements creating ripples that caught the early morning light. A Scrub Jay, the only bird species endemic to Florida, was watching closely as well. "What brought them back?" Chip asked.

"You did. When you removed the construction equipment and restored the natural water flow, you essentially sent out an invitation. Our Florida mangroves and pines have an incredible capacity for healing, but they need space and time." She pointed to a cluster of oysters growing on the mangrove roots. "See those? They're natural water filters. Each oyster can clean up to fifty gallons of water per day."

"Fifty gallons?" Chip knelt down to examine the small, unremarkable-looking mollusks. "I had no idea something so small could have such a big impact."

"That's the thing about ecosystem restoration," Dr. Lancaster said, making notes on her waterproof tablet. "Every component matters. Remove one piece, and the whole system can collapse. Restore one piece, and everything else starts to recover."

They continued their survey, moving deeper into the maze of channels that had once been marked for dredging. Chip had learned to read the subtle signs that Dr. Lancaster pointed out: the return of native grasses, the increasing bird diversity, the gradual clearing of water that had been murky for decades.

"I've been thinking," Chip said, as they paused to photograph a Roseate Spoonbill in the shallows, "about expanding this model to other sites."

Dr. Lancaster looked up from her camera. "Oh, what do you have in mind?"

"My family's company has been involved in dozens of developments throughout South Florida over the years. Not all of them were as environmentally destructive as this one almost was, but I'm starting to wonder how many opportunities we missed to do better."

"Are you thinking about retrofitting existing developments?"

"Maybe. Or possibly finding ways to incorporate restoration into new projects from the beginning." Chip watched a yellow-crowned night heron strike with lightning precision, emerging with a fish in its beak. "What if development and conservation didn't have to be opposing forces?"

Dr. Lancaster smiled. "Now you're thinking like a true restoration ecologist. There's actually a whole field called reconciliation ecology, finding ways for human development and natural systems to coexist."

"I want to learn more about that."

"I can recommend some reading. But if you're

serious about this, you should consider the program at FIU. They have an excellent Environmental Studies department, and they're always looking for students with real world experience."

Chip's head started swimming with this thought from the second she said it. He had taken a gap year after graduating to work on the WBRP, but he knew his family still expected him to attend one of the many prestigious universities available to him with the Waverly family name. But this idea about studying environmental and marine life at FIU had already planted itself in his brain like one of those mangrove seeds they'd been watching take root in the mud. College had always been the next step in his life plan, but he'd figured he'd study business or finance, maybe follow in his dad's footsteps. He'd never imagined studying something that would actually make him care this much.

"Chip, did you hear me?" Dr. Lancaster said, after seeing his face turn into a thousand-yard stare for at least 30 seconds.

"Loud and clear Dr. Lancaster. Loud and clear."

12

THE STUDENT

When looking at universities, what bothered Chip the most was having to be anywhere for 4 years, especially studying something he wasn't that interested in to begin with. Now, more than ever, he didn't want to be away from his beloved Wahoo Bay for that long. The accelerated program to achieve a degree in Environmental Sustainability in 1 year at FIU changed all that. He could now enhance his real-world experience, and back it up with an accredited degree, which he was certain would help him have more impact in the future with his environmental mission.

Chip's first day of classes at Florida International University felt completely surreal. For the first time in basically forever, it was just him, no Jake and no Tanner. At Nineteen, he was just a little older than most of his classmates, and his brief stint helping with his family's development business made him stick out like a sore thumb in a program packed with biology majors and hardcore environmental activists. Most of these kids had been saving sea turtles since middle school, not having their families plan to build condos on top of them. But as he sat in Dr. Jennifer Reyes's Ecosystem Restoration seminar, listening to her explain the complex relationships between hydrology, soil chemistry, and plant communities, he felt a familiar excitement, the same feeling he'd experienced during those early morning surveys at Wahoo Bay. And all those times in the morning with his sister, Sloan, about to go and discover new underwater species. It must have had an effect on him.

"Restoration isn't just about bringing back what was lost," Dr. Reyes explained, gesturing to a diagram of the Everglades' historical water flow. "It's about understanding why it was lost in the first place, and addressing those root causes."

An exchange student from The Bahamas raised her hand. "But what about economic factors? Isn't that one of the biggest root causes? Most environmental destruction happens because ultimately, restoration just isn't profitable."

"That's exactly the challenge," Dr. Reyes replied. "Which is why we need people who understand both ecology and economics. Anyone have thoughts on that?"

It was unbelievable that his first day at FIU, this was the first topic of conversation, and even more unbelievably, Chip found himself speaking before he'd consciously decided to. "What if we stopped thinking of restoration as a cost, and started thinking of it as an investment? The Wahoo Bay project is generating more revenue over time than the original condo development would have, and it's sustainable long-term."

The class turned to look at him, and Chip felt the familiar flutter of being put on the spot, but Dr. Reyes nodded encouragingly.

"Can you elaborate on that?"

"Well, luxury condos are a one-time sale. You build them, sell them, and then you're done. But eco-tourism, research partnerships, educational programs, those generate ongoing revenue streams. Plus, they increase property values in surrounding areas without destroying the ecosystem that makes those areas valuable in the first place."

A student with hair the color of a periwinkle flower leaned forward. "But that only works if you can convince developers to think long-term instead of chasing quick profits."

"True," Chip admitted, "but what if we could show them that the long-term profits are actually bigger? My family's company stock price has tripled since we pivoted to conservation. Environmental funds are fighting to invest in us."

Dr. Reyes smiled. "This is exactly the kind of thinking we need more of. Chip, would you be interested in presenting a case study on the Wahoo Bay project to the class next week?"

"Umm, yes, sure, of course," Chip replied, clearly caught a little off guard.

After class, the nearly lavender-haired, green-eyed student, who introduced herself as Maya Hudson, caught up with him in the hallway. "I have to admit, when you first started talking, I thought you were going to be another green washing corporate type. But that was actually pretty insightful."

"Thanks, I think?"

Maya laughed. "It's a compliment. I'm working on my thesis about community-based conservation in urban areas. Mind if I ask you something?"

"Sure."

"How did you convince your family to give up millions in guaranteed profits for a restoration project that might not work?"

Chip thought about the question as they walked

toward the parking lot. "Honestly? I don't think I convinced them of anything. The pelicans did that."

"The pelicans?"

"It's a long story. But basically, we learned that sometimes the natural world has its own ways of getting your attention."

"Oh really? Well, do you think the pelicans could convince a few other business magnates out there to change their ways?" she said, halfway joking, still trying to imagine how pelicans influenced corporate decision-making.

"Well, I can certainly talk to them next time I see them," Chip said with a laugh, while still seriously considering the prospect.

13

THE THESIS

Six months into his college program, Chip had found his academic calling. His thesis project, titled, "Blue Economic Models for Profitable Ecosystem Restoration," was attracting attention from professors across multiple departments. Dr. Reyes had connected him with economists, urban planners, and even a few business school faculty who were intrigued by his hybrid approach.

The research was consuming, but in the best possible way. Chip spent his mornings at Wahoo Bay collecting data on visitor numbers, revenue streams, and ecological indicators. His afternoons were devoted to analyzing similar projects across the state, building economic models that could predict the long-term profitability of restoration versus traditional development.

The preliminary results were encouraging. In case after case, restoration projects that survived their initial funding phases went on to generate more sustainable revenue than the developments they replaced. The key was finding the right mix of eco-tourism, research partnerships, educational programs, and carbon credit sales.

"Your data is solid," Dr. Reyes said during one of their weekly meetings, "but I think you're missing something important."

"What's that?"

"The human element. You're treating this like a purely economic question, but restoration is fundamentally about relationships, between people and land, between communities and ecosystems, between present needs and future sustainability."

She pulled out a map of South Florida, marked with dozens of pins representing various development projects. "Each of these sites has a story. Some are success stories like Wahoo Bay; others are cautionary tales. But they all involve people making choices about how to relate to the natural world."

"You think I should interview people? Like oral history?"

"I think you should understand the decision-making process that leads to restoration versus destruction. What makes some developers choose preservation, while others choose immediate profit? What role do communities play? How do cultural factors influence these choices?"

The suggestion sent Chip's research in an entirely new direction. Over the following weeks, he conducted interviews with developers, tribal leaders, environmental activists, coral restoration facilities, and community members throughout South Florida. The stories that emerged were complex, often surprising, and sometimes heartbreaking.

- *The Miami developer who had spent twenty years building luxury high-rises before a near-death experience led him to dedicate his remaining years to wetland restoration.*

- *The Seminole tribal council that had successfully blocked three separate development projects through a combination of legal challenges and public pressure campaigns.*

- *The community group in the Keys that had raised two million dollars to purchase and preserve a critical bird nesting area that was slated for resort development.*

But perhaps the most compelling story came from an unexpected source, Patricia Hensworth's own journey from investment banker to conservation advocate.

"I spent thirty years moving money around, making rich people richer," she told Chip during a long interview at the Wahoo Bay visitor center. "I was good at it, but I was miserable. When I learned about your great-great-grandfather, his findings showed me that money could be a tool for healing instead of just accumulation."

The interview crystallized something Chip had been struggling to articulate in his thesis. Restoration wasn't just about economics or ecology, it was about legacy, about the stories future generations would tell about the choices made today.

Chip's thesis defense was scheduled for a humid Thursday morning in late April, exactly two years after the pelican uprising that had changed everything. The examining committee included Dr. Reyes, two economists from the business school, an anthropologist who specialized in indigenous land rights, and Dr. Blackwater, who had been granted special status as a community expert.

The presentation room was packed beyond capacity. Word had spread about the "Pelican Pointe guy" who was trying to prove that conservation could be profitable. Maya Hudson sat in the front row, having become both a close friend and fierce intellectual sparring partner over the past year.

Jake, Tanner, Uncle Marcus, Aunt Kim, and his own mother and father, plus both sisters occupied seats near the back, looking proud.

"The traditional model of land development," Chip began, clicking to his first slide, "treats natural ecosystems as obstacles to be overcome rather than assets to be preserved. My research suggests this is not only environmentally destructive, but economically shortsighted."

He walked the committee through two years of data from Wahoo Bay: visitor numbers that had exceeded projections by 300%, research partnerships that generated steady rental income, and educational programs booked solid through the following year, not to mention the carbon credit sales. Jake and Tanner had taken full-time positions as co-partners while Chip was studying. They weren't far from each other geographically, but their packed schedules made it feel like an ocean's width apart.

"But the economic benefits extend beyond the immediate site," Chip continued, advancing to a map showing property values in the surrounding area. "Homes within a five-mile radius of Wahoo Bay have appreciated 15% faster than comparable properties elsewhere in the county. The presence of protected natural areas creates what economists call a 'halo effect,' which is to say an increased desirability that benefits the entire region."

Dr. Martinez, one of the business school economists, raised her hand. "Your model assumes continued growth in eco-tourism and environmental education. What happens if those markets become saturated?"

"That's where the diversification comes in," Chip replied, clicking to his next slide.

"The research station generates income through university partnerships, government contracts, and private research agreements. The carbon credit market is expanding rapidly as more companies seek to offset their emissions. And we're developing new revenue streams constantly. Last month, we launched a sustainable aquaculture program that's already showing promise."

The questions continued for over an hour, covering everything from statistical methodology to the replicability of the Wahoo Bay model. But the most challenging question came from Dr. Blackwater.

"Your research focuses heavily on economic incentives," she said, "but what about the cultural and spiritual dimensions of land stewardship? How do you quantify the value of sacred sites or the cost of cultural destruction?"

Chip had been preparing for this question for months. "You can't quantify those values in traditional economic terms, and you shouldn't try. But you can incorporate them into decision-making frameworks by recognizing that some forms of value transcend market calculations."

He clicked to a slide showing the Wahoo Bay covenant, the document that had started everything. "My great-great-grandfather understood that his role wasn't to own this land, but to protect it. That's not an economic relationship; it's a moral one. But paradoxically, honoring that moral obligation has turned out to be more economically beneficial than treating the land as a commodity."

The defense concluded with unanimous approval and congratulations from the committee. As the crowd dispersed, Chip felt a profound sense of completion, not just of his degree, but of a journey that had transformed his understanding of success, responsibility, and what it meant to be a Waverly. Chip was looking forward to getting back upcoast to Hillsboro Inlet, to the beach house, his family, and of course, those Wahoo Bay pelicans!

14

BACK ON THE WATER

Three weeks after his thesis defense, Chip found himself exactly where he wanted to be, standing on the deck of his new Jupiter Offshore boat, watching Jake bait a hook with ballyhoo, using the focused intensity of a surgeon. The boat was a graduation gift from his father, a sleek center console that could handle both the Intracoastal and the deep water of the Atlantic, where the big ones lived. Just like old times!

"You sure you remember how to do this?" Tanner called from the bow, where he was rigging a big game hook ballyhoo with practiced ease. "It's been what, two years since you've been fishing?"

"Like riding a bike," Chip replied, though privately he wondered if that was true. The past two years had been consumed with research, classes, and the constant demands of the restoration project. He'd barely touched a fishing rod since the day he'd first met Dr. Blackwater at the cultural center.

The morning was perfect for fishing: overcast skies that would keep the fish active, light winds that barely rippled the surface, and that particular quality of light that made the water look like deep blue glass. They'd launched from the Wahoo Bay marina, a small facility that had been built on the island as part of the restoration project to provide access for researchers and eco-tourists.

"First cast goes to the graduate," Jake announced, trolling some wake. "Let's see if all that book learning affected your arm."

Chip picked up his rod with a Penn setup that felt both familiar and foreign in his hands. It is built for fishing monsters. The only monsters he had a grip on over the last two years were Ticonderoga pencils.

"Not a bad reel for a college boy," Tanner remarked, which was his own cousinly way of congratulating Chip on graduating.

"So, what's next?" Jake asked, working his own

lure on the boat's back basin. "You gonna be Dr. Chip now, telling everyone how to save the world?"

"I don't know," Chip admitted. "I've got some job offers, consulting firms that want to hire me to help other developers pivot to conservation, taking advantage of new blue economy incentives. But I'm not sure that's what I want to do."

"What do you want to do?"

Before Chip could answer, his rod bent sharply, and the line began screaming off his reel. "Fish on!" he shouted, more from excitement than necessity. Jake and Tanner could clearly see the rod doubled over and the tense line vibrating over the surface of the water, indicating that something large had taken his bait.

"That's a good one," Tanner said, moving to clear the other lines. "Keep your rod tip up and let the drag do the work."

The fish made a powerful run toward deeper water, and Chip felt the familiar thrill of being connected to something wild and strong. This was what he'd missed during his academic years, the immediate, visceral connection to the natural world that no amount of research could replicate.

The battle lasted thirty minutes, with the fish making several determined runs before finally allowing itself to be worked toward the boat. As it came into view, all three men let out appreciative whistles.

"That's a Florida Blackfin Tuna if I ever saw one," Jake said, readying the net. "Thirty-eight inches, maybe forty!"

The fish was beautiful: black and silver with a distinctive black, sharp tail. Its slick skin in the sunlight looked like polished metal. Chip felt a surge of pure joy as he put his head almost into the water to look at it up close before taking the hook out and releasing it.

"Perfect eating size," Tanner observed, but Chip was already shaking his head.

"I put him back. He needs to multiply."

Jake looked at him with surprise. "Since when do you catch and release?"

"Since I learned what it takes to bring fish populations back from the brink," Chip replied, carefully removing the hook and cradling the silver and black beauty in the water. "This guy probably took three years to reach this size. In the old days, before the restoration, there weren't many tuna in these waters at all."

He watched the fish recover for a moment, its gills working steadily, before it gave a powerful thrust of its tail and disappeared into the petrol blue depths.

"You've changed, man," Jake said, but there was respect in his voice.

"Yeah, I have." Chip reeled in his line and looked towards the beach where his family's home sat, with the clear water, and the Terns shuffling along on the shoreline. "And I think I know what I want to do next."

"What's that?"

"I want to start a company. Not a development company like our family's always run, but something different. A restoration company that helps other landowners make the same choice we made."

Tanner raised an eyebrow. "You think there's a market for that?"

"I think there's a need for it. And I think the market is about to catch up." Jake toggled a new ballyhoo on the line and Chip dropped it into the drink. "Climate change, sea level rise, hurricane damage, all of these things are making traditional coastal development riskier and more expensive. Insurance companies are starting to refuse coverage for projects in vulnerable areas."

"So, you'd help people turn their land into nature preserves?"

"Not exactly. I'd help them find ways to develop that work with natural systems instead of against them: elevated construction that allows water flow, native landscaping that provides habitat, stormwater management that mimics natural processes." The ideas had been percolating in his mind for months, but speaking them aloud made them feel real and urgent.

"What would you call this company?" Jake asked.

Chip thought for a moment, "Pelican Partners," he said finally, "in honor of the birds that taught us everything we needed to know about standing your ground."

The morning continued with steady fishing, a few more tuna, several spotted grouper, and a small sailfish that Jake managed to land (but then release) after a spectacular jumping fight. But Chip found his mind wandering to business plans and partnership possibilities, to the dozen or so developers who had already reached out asking for advice on their own projects.

By noon, the sun had broken through the clouds, and the fish had moved to deeper water. They headed back toward the marina, the boat cutting smoothly through water that was clearer than Chip remembered from his childhood fishing trips.

"You know what's funny?" he said as they approached the dock. "Two years ago, I thought my life was falling apart. The pelican attacks, the failed development, Aunt Kim's racoon raid, it all felt awful."

"And now?" Tanner asked.

"Now I realize it was all preparation. Every setback was actually pointing me toward something better." He gestured toward the thriving ecosystem around them, the research station visible in the distance, the small boats full of eco-tourists exploring the mangrove channels. "Sometimes you have to lose everything you thought you wanted to discover what you actually need."

As they tied up at the marina, Chip noticed a familiar figure waiting on the dock, Dr. Blackwater, holding what appeared to be an official-looking document.

"Chip" she called out with a smile. "I was hoping I'd find you here. I have some news that I think you'll find interesting."

"Good news or bad news?"

"That depends on how you feel about expanding your restoration model to the Caribbean."

Chip felt his pulse quicken. "What do you mean?" Jake and Tanner were all ears as well.

"The Bahamian government has been following the Wahoo Bay project. They're dealing with similar pressures: over development, ecosystem destruction, climate change impacts. They want to hire you to help them develop a national restoration strategy."

"Looks like 'Pelican Partners' is ready to be launched!" said Jake, looking over at Chip excitedly.

Dr. Blackwater laughed. "Then I suggest you incorporate quickly. They want to meet with you next month, and they're prepared to offer a very substantial contract."

Chip was on stun. "Next month? It's all happening so fast, and I'm thrilled, but…why me, why us? Our average age isn't even 20, and we've just been doing this for 2 years."

"Perhaps they recognize that our hope for the future is in our youth. We can't move forward with old ideas that aren't serving us anymore. They want new ideas, ones that you are already proving can fix the environmental problems of today and those that are ahead. So get ready!" Dr. Blackwater said to him proudly as she left Chip to think about this new opportunity.

As Chip stood on the dock under an amber lantern, salt water still dripping from his clothes, and the sting of the salt on his bronzed skin, he felt the same sense of rightness that had guided him through the past two years. The path ahead was uncertain, but it was his path, carved out through a combination of accident, determination, and the wisdom of birds who knew when to fight and when to fly.

"Jake, Tanner," he said, turning to his cousins who were still securing the boat. "How would you feel about taking a trip to the Bahamas? I think I might need some partners who know their way around the water."

Jake looked up from coiling a dock line. "You serious?"

"Dead serious. If we're going to help restore

marine ecosystems, I need people who understand how they actually work. People who've spent their lives reading water, following fish, understanding the connections between different habitats."

Tanner straightened up, interest flickering in his eyes.

"What kind of work are we talking about?"

"The kind that matters," Chip replied. "The kind that makes a difference."

15

THE PROPOSAL

Two weeks later, Jake found himself in an unfamiliar environment, the office at the Wahoo Bay Research Station, wearing his one good button-down shirt, and trying not to fidget with his phone. Across the table sat Dr. Blackwater, Patricia Hensworth, and a woman named Dr. Julia Mae Rolle, a native Bahamian, who had flown in from Nassau to discuss the Bahamas project.

Jake was usually the hands-on crew member. Tanner and Chip were there as well. They were a little more at home with the buttoned-up work.

"The challenge we're facing," Dr. Rolle explained,

pulling up satellite images on her laptop, "is that traditional conservation approaches aren't working fast enough. We're losing coral reefs, seagrass beds, and mangrove forests faster than we can protect them through legislation alone."

Tanner leaned forward, studying the images. "What's causing the damage? It looks like what we have here, but please tell us more."

"There are multiple factors: coastal development, agricultural runoff, overfishing, climate change. But the biggest problem is how local communities view conservation. They think that either we conserve the environment and hurt the economy, or we develop the economy and hurt the environment. Ultimately, they're worried about providing for their families."

Jake nodded. "Same thing that happened here. People need to make a living. The blue economy dynamic actually works."

"Exactly. Which is why we're interested in the Wahoo Bay model. You've proven that restoration can be profitable, but more importantly, you've shown how to get local communities invested in the process. Your team has transformed the fake reef installation process, and came up with a larger, more efficient and natural reef."

Chip clicked to the next slide, showing photos from their recent fishing trip. "Jake and Tanner aren't just fishing guides, they're ecosystem monitors. They notice changes in fish populations, water quality, and habitat conditions before any scientific instrument could detect them."

"We've been thinking," Tanner said, his usual reticence giving way to enthusiasm, "about ways to make conservation more, you know, active. More hands-on."

Dr. Rolle raised an eyebrow. "What do you mean?" she asked in her breezy Bahamian accent.

Jake pulled out his iPad, and showed a video he'd shot the previous week.

"We were fishing near some coral heads that had been severely damaged by boat propellers," Jake said, while Dr. Rolle closely studied the footage. "Tanner proposed an intriguing idea: what if we could expand on the development of advanced artificial reefs that not only mimic the ecological functions of natural reefs, but also effectively divert boats away from the fragile ecosystems? With cutting-edge technologies like 3D printing and eco-friendly materials, we could create structures that promote marine life, while also drawing more boaters to them instead of the natural reefs that are much more fragile. These innovative reefs could incorporate features like strategically-placed underwater gardens and unique shapes that draw in fish, turning them into vibrant hotspots for marine biodiversity, all while protecting the natural coral from further harm. We want there to be a positive return for the ocean as well as us!"

Jake then transitioned to another video, an animated example, showcasing what they could build. This video unveiled a mesmerizing underwater structure crafted from uniquely designed concrete blocks, their surfaces rough and textured, creating a perfect habitat for marine life. This architectural marvel boasted multiple levels, each tier cascading downwards like a submerged staircase, already bustling with small fish darting in and out of the crevices. Sunlight filtered through the crystalline water, illuminating the vibrant scene as the structure began to show signs of coral growth, delicate tendrils of color emerging like nature's artwork, painting the blocks with hues of pink, orange, and purple.

"We refer to them as 'sacrifice reefs,'" Tanner explained, his eyes glimmering with enthusiasm. "These innovative structures are meticulously designed with multiple tiers, enhancing their appeal to recreational fishermen far beyond that of the natural reefs. Strategically placed in locations where boat traffic poses no threat of destruction, they serve as artificial sanctuaries for marine life. We are truly grateful for the robust community of coral reef revivers dedicated to this cause, yet we find ourselves in need of methods to accelerate their growth and fortify their resilience, ensuring a thriving underwater ecosystem."

"With that in mind, we would like to build a modular artificial reef system designed for marine habitat restoration. The structure would consist of interlocking components that can be customized based on local marine conditions and species needs." Tanner motioned back to his video presentation, where individual slides highlight the proposed structure.

Key features include:

- *Multi-level vertical structures with varying ledge depths*

- *Protected nursery spaces for juvenile fish*

- *Elevated hunting platforms for apex predators*

- *Hurricane-resistant anchoring system*

- *Expandable design allowing for ecosystem growth*

- *Specialized "sacrifice reef" components that redirect pressure from natural reefs*

"The materials used are environmentally inert, and designed to promote marine growth while maintaining structural integrity in saltwater conditions."

"This is brilliant," Dr. Rolle said, pausing the video to examine the structure more closely. "Have you tested the concept?"

"We've got a dozen or so of them deployed around Wahoo Bay near the park on the inlet," Jake replied. "Fish populations are up 40% in the surrounding areas, and we've documented a 60% reduction in propeller scars on the natural reefs."

Patricia was beaming, as the boys told of their great success with Wahoo Bay Island, and Dr. Rolle leaned in, showing a growing interest and excitement with every word.

Chip went on to state, "Originally developed at The Wahoo Bay Restoration Project, this system evolved through collaboration with fishermen, marine biologists, and environmental engineers. Early prototypes focused on basic habitat creation, but the design rapidly evolved to include specialized features for different species and ecological roles. The success at Wahoo Bay can lead to adaptation for Caribbean waters, where further refinements would be made based on local conditions and species requirements. Perhaps it can be known as the "Wahoo Bay Protocol!"

Patricia Hensworth leaned back in her chair, a satisfied grin on her face. "Gentlemen, I believe you've just made significant strides toward addressing one of the Caribbean's most pressing conservation issues."

The weight of the task ahead loomed large, as they would need to navigate complex ecosystems, engage local communities, and secure funding against a backdrop of climate change and dwindling resources. Each step of the project would require careful planning, collaboration, and unwavering commitment to truly make a difference in preserving the region's fragile environment.

"But that's just the beginning," Tanner continued. "We've been working on designs for floating nursery habitats that can be deployed in areas where natural nurseries have been destroyed, and Jake's got this crazy idea for underwater viewing stations that would let tourists observe marine life without disturbing it."

Jake's grin spread widely across his face, his eyes sparkling with enthusiasm. "It's not crazy; it's practical! Just imagine it, rather than having people donning masks and flippers, snorkeling over delicate coral reefs and inadvertently harming them, they could experience the wonders of the underwater world from enclosed viewing pods. These pods would allow for safe observation without any physical contact with the fragile ecosystem!"

Dr. Blackwater had been quiet throughout the presentation, but now she spoke up.

"What you're describing is a completely new approach to conservation."

Dr. Rolle nodded with excitement. "This all sounds so wonderful, and exactly what we need!"

"We're so glad you think so!" Chip replied. "Is there anything else you would like to go over, or anyone else we need to meet with to help get the ball rolling?"

"Not at all. I was already given full power as a representative of the Bahamian government to green light your proposal, if it was satisfactory...and it is! We'd like you to kick things off on Andros Island, it's our biggest island and has the most pressing conservation issues. When can you get started?"

16

ISLAND ARRIVAL•TIME TO GET SERIOUS!

The seaplane banked sharply over the turquoise waters of the Tongue of the Ocean, giving Chip a breath-taking aerial view of Andros Island. From two thousand feet, the island looked like a green jewel set in impossible blue, its western shore indented with countless creeks and bays that reminded him of the Florida Keys.

"Holy moly!" Jake muttered, pressing his face to the small window. "Look at the size of that blue hole."

Tanner craned his neck to see past his brother. "That's got to be three hundred feet across."

The pilot, a seasoned Bahamian named Captain Jack Pinder, chuckled over the intercom.

"Behold the Andros Blue Hole, the vast underwater cave that plunges deeper than any other in the Caribbean, descending over six hundred feet into an unforgiving darkness. Local fishermen whisper tales of its eerie depths, claiming it is cursed, haunted by the restless spirits of sailors who met a watery grave, eternally wandering the depths in search of escape."

"Fun," Tanner said in a most satirical way.

As they descended for their water landing at Andros Town, Chip felt a familiar mixture of excitement and apprehension. The Wahoo Bay project had been challenging enough, but at least it was in familiar territory. Here, they were dealing with different ecosystems, different communities, different political realities.

"You nervous?" Tanner asked, noticing Chip's white-knuckled grip on the armrest.

"Terrified," Chip admitted. "What if we can't replicate what we did in Florida? What if the conditions are too different?"

"Then we adapt," Jake said simply. "Fish are fish, water is water. The principles are the same even if the details change."

The Tropic Ocean Airways flight was only one hour from Fort Lauderdale, and the boys were excited to get on their way to Small Hope Bay Beach, just north of Fresh Creek. It's known for its proximity to the Tongue of the Ocean, and is situated about 20 miles west of Nassau. It's also famous for bonefish angling and beautiful flats water.

As they exited the plane, the heat enveloped them like a tangible weight, the humid, salt-laden air making their Florida summer feel mild in comparison. It was such a short distance away, but it was a world apart.

A small delegation was waiting for them: Dr. Rolle, looking crisp and professional despite the heat, and a tall, Bahamian man in khaki shorts and a fishing shirt who introduced himself as Bonefish Charlie, their local guide, plus a local woman wearing a traditional, almost junkanoo, colorful headwrap, who stepped forward with a warm smile.

"Welcome to Andros," she said, extending her hand. "I'm Delores Albury, president of the Andros Conservancy. We've been following your work in Florida with great interest."

"Thank you for having us," Chip replied, shaking her hand. "We're honored to be here."

"Feeling honored and a bit sweaty," Jake said, using his sleeve to wipe his brow.

Delores chuckled. "No need to fret; once we get you out on the water, the trade winds will cool you down."

They loaded their equipment into a battered

pickup truck, and drove through Andros Town, a collection of colorful concrete buildings that seemed to shimmer in the heat. Children waved from doorways, and Chip noticed several boats pulled up on the beach that looked like they'd been there for decades.

"The entire fishing industry here is struggling," Dr. Rolle explained as they drove. "Overfishing, habitat destruction, competition from commercial operations. Many of the traditional fishing families are barely making ends meet."

"Which is why they're skeptical of conservation efforts," Delores added. "They've heard promises before about sustainable fishing and eco-tourism, but they've never seen the benefits materialize."

Bonefish Charlie spoke up, with his salty, local Bahamian accent, from the driver's seat. "My grandfadda, he fish dese waters for seventy years, ya know. He used to tell stories 'bout bonefish so thick you could walk 'cross dey backs, grouper big as bathtubs, lobster e'rywhere you look. Now my boy, he gotta go farder and farder out just to catch nuff fish to feed his family."

They pulled up to a small marina where a thirty-foot Mako flat bottom skiff was tied to the dock, reminding Chip of his beloved skiff at home. The boat was well maintained, with custom rod holders and a tower that suggested serious fishing credentials.

"Dis our ride," Charlie announced. "She is pretty, and she knows dese waters better den any GPS."

As they loaded their gear, Chip noticed a group of neighborhood fishermen watching from the shade of a nearby conch shack. Their expressions ranged from curious to skeptical, and one older man shook his head dismissively when he saw the Americans unloading their equipment.

"Don't mind them," Delores said quietly. "They've seen plenty of outsiders come through with big promises. You'll have to prove yourselves on the water before they'll take you seriously."

The boat ride to their first survey site took them through a maze of shallow creeks and mangrove channels that reminded Chip powerfully of home. But the water here was clearer, almost gin-clear in places, and the colors were more intense, emerald green in the shallows, deep sapphire in the channels, and that impossible electric blue where the bottom dropped away into the abyss.

"First stop is what we call de Nursery," Charlie explained, throttling back as they approached a shallow bay surrounded by mangroves. "Used to be thick with juvenile fish: snappers, groupers, grunts. Now, not so good," he gestured at the water, which looked eerily empty.

Jake leaned over the side, studying the bottom.

"Sea grass is patchy. Looks like prop scars, but also clear signs of a sargassum die-off."

"Sargassum blooms, similar to those in Florida and Mexico," Dr. Rolle confirmed. "These enormous algae blooms obstruct sunlight and diminish oxygen levels. They have been worsening each year with rising sea temperatures. We are facing a global seaweed crisis."

Jake went on to elaborate while studying the sea floor, "While Sargassum seaweed plays an essential role in the open ocean, it becomes problematic when it overwhelms coastlines, disrupting ecosystems, economies, and the overall public health. Significant accumulations can suffocate coral reefs, reduce oxygen in coastal waters leading to fish die-offs, and emit harmful gases, such as hydrogen sulfide during decomposition, which can cause breathing difficulties and unpleasant odors. Additionally, the seaweed obstructs beaches, and clogs waterways."

Dr. Rolle knew she had brought over the right people to help.

Tanner was already assembling his underwater camera equipment. "Mind if I take a look?"

"Be my guest. But watch out for the barracuda, they're curious about shiny objects." The boys knew that already, but nodded and waved out of respect.

For the next hour, they conducted their first survey of Andros waters. The results were sobering.

Fish populations were dramatically lower than historical records suggested, coral reefs showed extensive bleaching and disease, and the sea grass beds that served as nurseries for juvenile fish were in serious decline.

But there were also signs of hope. In areas where local fishing pressure had been reduced, either through informal community agreements or natural barriers to access, marine life was noticeably more abundant. The ecosystem's capacity for recovery was still there; it just needed the right conditions.

"The good news," Chip said as they headed back to the marina, "is that the fundamental structure is intact. The mangroves, the reef systems, the deep-water connections, they're all still functional. What we're seeing is degradation, not collapse."

"Can dey be fixed?" Charlie asked.

"I think so. But it's going to take a different approach than what we used in Florida. Here, we need to work with the fishing communities, not around them."

That evening, they gathered at Delores' house for dinner and their first community meeting. The living room was packed with fishermen, their wives, local business owners, and several teenagers who seemed more interested than expected.

"The problem, y'know," said a grizzled, island fisherman named Winston, "is dat every time someone comes 'round here talkin' 'bout conservation, it means less fishin', less money, less work for we people. How dis gonna be any different, eh?"

Chip had been expecting this question. "Because we're not here to stop fishing. We're here to help you catch more fish."

The room fell silent. Winston raised an eyebrow. "Come again?"

"The artificial reefs we've developed in Florida have increased fish populations by 40% in surrounding areas. The floating nursery habitats we're designing could restore juvenile fish populations to historical levels. We're not talking about restricting fishing, we're talking about creating more fish to catch. It's called 'Blue Economy,' and has many ways to create a living while helping keep this lifestyle and community alive."

"And how do we know this isn't just more promises?" asked a woman named Grace, whose husband ran a small fishing charter business.

Jake stood up. "Because we're fishermen too. Everything we're proposing, we've tested ourselves. We have embraced the hard work and results from other like-minded ocean conservationists. We look and we listen. We have gone to bat with these teams against the Florida government and won. We know it works because we've seen it work."

He pulled out his phone and showed videos from

their recent trips around Wahoo Bay Island, through the inlet and out to open waters: healthy reefs, abundant fish, successful fishing charters operating in harmony with conservation efforts.

"The key," Tanner added, "is that fishermen become partners in the restoration, not obstacles to it. You know these waters better than any scientist. You notice changes before anyone else. That knowledge is invaluable."

The meeting continued past midnight, with increasingly animated discussions about specific locations, fishing techniques, and potential solutions. By the time people started heading home, Chip sensed a cautious optimism that hadn't been there at the beginning of the evening.

"Not bad for a first meeting," Delores said as the last guests departed. "You managed to get Winston talking, and he hasn't said more than two words at a community meeting in five years."

"He reminds me of the Miccosukee tribe back home," Chip replied, walking out with Delores. "Suspicious of any outsiders, but passionate about wildlife. Those are the people you need on your side if you want real change."

Just then, beneath a vast expanse of night sky shimmering with countless stars, a pod of pelicans soared overhead in a flawless V formation, their wings outstretched against the dark canvas of the heavens. "A good omen," Chip mused silently to himself, feeling a sense of hope swell within him as he prepared to embark on this next pivotal stage of his environmental mission.

17

FIRST DEPLOYMENT

Three weeks into their Andros residency, the team was ready to deploy their first artificial reef system. They'd spent the intervening time conducting detailed surveys, and bringing on volunteers from Florida and the Caribbean for the reef ball installation. It takes time, money and human help to build each piece of the construction.

They put out a call to action for volunteers:

HELP WITH MULTIPLE

VITAL INSTALLATIONS!

The ad read:

The project involves pouring concrete into molds, then taking apart the reef ball molds that were previously poured using hammers, reassembling these molds, and pouring marine friendly concrete into a fiberglass mold to create reef balls. These reef balls will be installed to stabilize and build reefs and prevent erosion while creating a habitat similar to natural fish communities found along coral suffering areas throughout the Caribbean. The specific shapes and designs of the building blocks vary.

Some common shapes include:

• Concrete balls and pyramids: These are designed to be cost-effective and provide shelter for smaller marine animals.

• Modular designs: Some artificial reefs utilize modular designs that create multiple habitats within a single structure.

- *Specialized blocks: Certain designs utilize special blocks to create specific effects like localized turbulence.*

- *ECOBLOX: custom 3d-printed concrete tiles that help restore biodiversity, reduce erosion, and bring back the oyster population (nature's water filters!).*

Please only wear closed-toe shoes and clothing that you don't mind getting dirty. Bring REEF SAFE SUNBLOCK ONLY! Yes, the Bahamas strongly encourages the use of reef-safe sunscreen. While not formally banned, the use of sunscreens containing oxybenzone and octinoxate is discouraged due to their potential harm to coral reefs. Mineral sunscreens with zinc oxide and titanium dioxide are recommended as safer alternatives. Used gloves will be provided, but bring your own if you prefer.

Other suggestions include wearing a hat, bug repellent, and bringing a water bottle. We will provide a large jug of ice water to refill your bottle. After orientation at the landing strip at Fresh Creek, meet us in the northern end of our lot where the project will be load-

ed. We will be installing fish reef balls, which weigh 200 pounds each. Two people share the weight of each reef ball at a time to go into the water to install it on the shoreline. This effort will help restore lost habitat by promoting new fish growth, ultimately improving water quality and providing food sources and habitat for many species.

We appreciate your help in this project that ultimately aims to revitalize your ecosystem, economy, and your entire community!

This was probably one of the most important pieces any of the boys had ever written, and it was a goombay smash, as they say in the Bahamas! It drew many ocean-loving individuals to this endeavor.

They were also meeting with fishing families, and adapting their Florida designs to Caribbean conditions. The result was a hybrid structure that combined elements of their original sacrifice reefs with features specifically designed for Bahamian species.

"De grouper here behave differently den Florida grouper," Charlie explained as they loaded the concrete modules onto his boat. "They like deeper ledges, more vertical structure. And de snappers school different, dey need more open space to move around."

Jake nodded, making notes on his waterproof tablet. "That's why we added the tower sections. Creates multiple depth zones in a single structure."

The deployment site was a sandy bottom area about two miles offshore, deep enough to avoid most boat traffic, but shallow enough for recreational fishing. More importantly, it was directly adjacent to a natural reef system that had been heavily damaged by a combination of bleaching events and physical destruction.

"The idea," Tanner explained to the small crowd of local fishermen who had come to watch, "is that the artificial reef formations will take pressure off the natural one while it recovers. Fish will use both areas, but the fishing pressure will concentrate on the artificial structure."

Winston, who had become an unlikely ally over the past few weeks, squinted at the concrete modules. "How long 'fore de fish start usin' it?"

"In Florida, we saw fish within hours of deployment," Chip replied. "but full colonization takes six months to a year."

The deployment itself was surprisingly straightforward. Using GPS coordinates and a small hand-crank crane mounted on a local flatbed barge that was donated for the day. Along with the multitude of young volunteers, they lowered each module to the seafloor with precision. The structures were designed to interlock, creating a complex three-dimensional habitat that would only become more attractive to marine life as coral and algae began to colonize the surfaces.

"There," Jake said as the final module disappeared beneath the surface. "Now we wait."

But they didn't have to wait long. Within an hour, Tanner's underwater camera was recording schools of yellowtail snappers investigating the new structures. By the end of the day, they'd documented sergeant majors, parrot fish, and several small grouper taking up residence in the artificial reef's crevices.

"I'll be damned," Winston muttered, watching the footage on Tanner's camera. "Dey moved in faster den dem tourists to a new Margaritaville!" The young team of volunteers agreed!

The triumphant success of the first deployment sparked an insatiable desire for more among the community. Within a mere month, they had strategically placed five intricately designed artificial reefs along the rugged western shoreline of Andros, each reef meticulously crafted to accommodate the unique species inhabiting its specific location. However, the most remarkable aspect wasn't just the reefs themselves; it was the unexpected emergence of a vibrant network of local individuals who became as invested in the project as the original team. This burgeoning brigade of passionate volunteers infused the community with a renewed sense of purpose and optimism. Fishermen, who were once solitary in their endeavors, began to take an active interest in monitoring the sites, diligently reporting their observations, and even defending the structures from those who sought to disrupt their delicate ecosystems.

"It looks like the fishermen are beginning to take responsibility for policing the sites themselves," Delores announced during one of their weekly progress meetings, her voice brimming with pride. "Just yesterday, Winston heroically chased off a group of tourists attempting to spear fish on the newly established reef. He insisted it was too precious a resource to allow anyone to jeopardize its integrity."

This kind of local participation was one of the most important aspects of the Waverly boys' plan. If the locals were not invested in taking part, it would have been doomed to fail. With their help though, the reefs truly stood a chance of regenerating.

18

THE NURSERY EFFECT

The boys were able to secure a coral-adorned house near Small Hope Bay to stay as long as needed, leaving Wahoo Bay in Dr. Lancaster's capable hands while they were away. Three months into their Andros project, the artificial reefs had become something none of them had quite anticipated, actual nurseries. Tanner's daily dive surveys revealed juvenile fish species that hadn't been documented in these waters for years.

"Look at this," he said, pulling up footage from the morning dive. The camera panned across a section of reef where dozens of baby Nassau grouper darted between the artificial structures. "These juveniles are using the crevices exactly like they would in a natural reef system."

Jake leaned over Tanner's laptop screen, his engineering mind already working. "The spacing between the modules is creating perfect hiding spots for the smaller fish. But we need to think about the next phase, what happens when they outgrow these spaces?"

That question led to Jake's most ambitious design yet: modular expansion units that could be added to existing reefs as fish populations grew. Each unit was engineered with larger openings and deeper caves, creating a graduated habitat system that could support fish throughout their entire life cycle.

Chip, meanwhile, had been tracking something that was equally important: the economic ripple effects. "The fishermen are reporting better catches in areas adjacent to the reefs," he told the team during their weekly meeting. "Winston's boat brought in thirty percent more snapper last week than the same week last year."

The data was compelling. The artificial reefs weren't just supporting marine life, they were creating spillover effects that benefited the entire local fishing economy. Chip's economic models showed that each reef would generate approximately $15,000 in additional fishing revenue annually, while costing only $8,000 to build and maintain.

The arrival of the sharks changed everything, in a wonderful way. Tanner spotted the first one during a routine survey dive: a pint-size Caribbean blacktip reef shark, gliding effortlessly through the intricate labyrinth of artificial structures, exuding the casual confidence of an apex predator claiming new territory. Its streamlined, torpedo-shaped body cut through the water with grace, the sunlight shimmering off its dark dorsal fin. Tanner's heart raced with excitement as he immediately contacted the Bimini Shark Lab, the world-renowned field station dedicated to the study of sharks.

Within hours, the lab sprang into action, organizing a field trip to meet with Tanner, Chip, and Jake. The anticipation was palpable as the team arrived, their enthusiasm infectious. Within days of their arrival, they worked diligently to set up Jake's underwater cameras, each click of the shutter echoing their eagerness. Everyone was thrilled to witness the stunning footage capturing regular visits from a vibrant array of shark species: the gentle nurse sharks, the sleek blacktip sharks, and even a few graceful rays that glided by like underwater dancers adding to the spectacle of this thriving marine ecosystem.

"This is exactly what we wanted," Tanner explained to a group of visiting marine biologists from the University of Miami hosted by his cousin, Sloan. "Sharks are indicator species. Their presence means the ecosystem is functioning at a high level."

But the sharks also presented a challenge that fell squarely into Jake's wheelhouse. The original reef structures, designed primarily for smaller fish, needed modifications to accommodate larger predators without compromising the habitat for juvenile species.

Jake's solution was elegant in its simplicity: elevated platforms that created a multi-story reef system. Sharks could patrol the upper levels while smaller fish maintained their protected spaces below. The engineering required precise calculations of water flow, structural integrity, and predator-prey dynamics.

"It's like designing an apartment building for fish," Jake explained to Chip as they reviewed the blueprints. "Everyone gets their own floor, but the whole building has to work together."

The modified reefs were an immediate success. Within two weeks of installation, Tanner documented hunting behavior that hadn't been seen in these waters for decades, sharks working together to herd schools of fish, creating feeding opportunities that benefited multiple species throughout the food chain.

19

THE BREEDING GROUNDS

Six months after the first deployment, Tanner made a discovery that would change the trajectory of their entire project. During a dawn dive at the northernmost reef site, his camera captured something extraordinary: a pair of Nassau grouper engaged in spawning behavior.

"They're breeding," he announced breathlessly as he surfaced, his excitement causing him to forget his usual scientific composure. "The grouper are actually using our reefs as spawning grounds."

The implications were staggering. Nassau grouper

had been so over fished in Bahamian waters that successful breeding events were rare. If their artificial reefs could support reproduction, they weren't just creating habitat, they were actively rebuilding fish populations.

Chip immediately recognized the economic significance. "Having a breeding population means sustainable fisheries," he told the team. "This isn't just conservation anymore; it's fisheries management with a direct economic return."

Jake's role became critical as they worked to optimize the reefs for breeding behavior. Spawning fish required specific conditions: water depth, current patterns, and substrate types that would protect eggs and larvae. His engineering background proved invaluable as he designed specialized breeding modules with carefully calculated flow dynamics and protective features.

The breeding success attracted attention from marine biologists across the Caribbean. Dr. Simone Roker from the Bahamas National Trust arrived to document the spawning events, bringing with her a team of graduate students and sophisticated monitoring equipment.

"What you've created here," she told the team after a week of intensive surveys, "is essentially a fish factory. But unlike aquaculture, this is producing wild fish that are rebuilding natural populations."

Tanner's documentation of the breeding cycles became the foundation for a research paper that would eventually be published in Marine Ecology Progress Series. But more immediately, it provided the scientific credibility that transformed their project from an interesting experiment into a proven conservation model.

The success of the breeding program also solved a problem that had been nagging at Chip: long-term sustainability. Breeding populations meant the reefs would continue to generate economic benefits for decades, creating a self-sustaining system that could support both conservation and community development.

"We're not just building reefs," Chip realized as he watched footage of juvenile fish emerging from the spawning sites. "We're building the foundation for an entire blue economy."

20

THE STORM OF CHANGE

Hurricane Thelma arrived with little warning. A black cloud sky was behind the shiny coconut palm fronds, as the last light from the Sun was sparkling on them. The palms were beginning to bow to the blow. The storm was spinning up from a tropical depression to a Category 3 in less than forty-eight hours. The team barely had enough time to secure their equipment, and head to the airport before the storm made landfall on Andros's northern coast. Unfortunately, they were past the point of evacuation.

From the bar at the end of the runway, which

was the only place at the airport with electricity, and was also thankfully made out of concrete block, they watched satellite images of the hurricane's eye passing directly over their project sites. The storm surge was predicted to reach fifteen feet, with sustained winds of 120 mph, more than enough to destroy everything they'd built over the past three months.

"Well," Jake said grimly, staring at the weather radar, "I guess we're about to find out how well our designs hold up to real-world conditions."

"The artificial reefs should be fine," Tanner said, in a more hopeful than certain tone. "They're designed to handle wave action. But the floating nursery habitats…"

He didn't need to finish the sentence. The floating structures, anchored in shallow bays around the island, were vulnerable to both wind and surge. If the anchoring systems failed, months of work would be scattered across the seafloor, or worse, washed up on shore as expensive debris.

The guys ended up hunkering down at the airport until the storm had passed. It was a wise decision, as the hurricane drew near, threatening clouds began to gather on the horizon, enveloping the island in darkness.

The winds began to whip through the palm trees, bending their trunks as if they were bowing to an unseen force. The ocean churned violently, waves crashing against the shore with a ferocity that resonated like a war drum, signaling the impending chaos. Residents watched anxiously from their bungalows, feeling both the thrill and dread of nature's power. The storm was predicted to skirt the island, but even the outer bands of its influence brought heavy rains and gusty winds that rattled shutters and sent debris swirling through the air.

As the hurricane's eye passed by, the island was overtaken by an eerie calm, a deceptive lull that gave a false sense of security. The waters receded momentarily, exposing the sandy bottom and revealing the remnants of marine life that had been displaced. Birds that had taken refuge from the storm began to emerge, circling above the tumultuous sea, only to be quickly swept back into the tempest. The sky darkened once more, and the wind picked up again, howling like a wild beast as the storm continued its path. Though the island had escaped the full brunt of the hurricane, it was clear that the aftermath would leave its mark, reshaping the landscape, and reminding everyone of the raw power of nature.

The storm passed as quickly as it had formed, leaving behind tranquil seas, and skies so clear they seemed artificial. At the airport, the runway was flooded and littered with debris, and Chip felt his stomach clench at the sight of the devastation.

Palm trees lay twisted and broken like discarded

toothpicks. The small marina where they'd launched their surveys was completely destroyed, with boats scattered inland like toys. The community center where they'd held their first meeting was missing its entire roof.

"No," Jake whispered as they surveyed the damage from the truck. "It looks like a war zone."

What troubled Chip the most was Charlie's response. The usually chatty guide had been completely silent since collecting them at the airstrip. Since they never managed to leave, they got a firsthand view of the destruction while waiting out the storm at the airport. Charlie navigated through the debris with a serious look on his face, indicating he was no stranger to such devastation. Nor were they.

They spent two days assessing the damage to their project sites. The artificial reefs had survived, the concrete structures were exactly where they'd been placed, now serving as shelter for fish displaced by the storm. But the floating nursery habitats were gone, their anchor lines snapped, the structures themselves nowhere to be found.

"Forty thousand dollars worth of equipment," Tanner said, staring at the empty water where their most promising habitat had been anchored. "Just gone."

"The insurance will cover it," Jake replied, but he could hear the uncertainty in his own voice. They'd been operating on a tight budget, and this setback would consume most of their remaining funds.

That evening, as they sat in what remained of Delores' house, the walls were intact, but the roof was a patchwork of blue tarps, Winston delivered the news that Chip had been dreading.

"Most of de fishing boats are damaged beyond repair," he said in his quiet, local accent. "The few dat made it through de storm are needed for rescue and supply runs. Nobody gon be fishing for months, maybe longer."

"What does that mean for the project?" Dr. Rolle asked via satellite phone from Nassau.

Chip looked around the room at the faces of people who had become more than research subjects, they'd become friends, partners, family. They were facing the loss of their homes, their livelihoods, their entire way of life. His conservation project suddenly seemed trivial by comparison.

"It means we need to go home," he said finally. "These people need to rebuild their lives, not worry about fish habitats."

"But the artificial reefs are working," Jake protested. "The fish populations are already recovering. We can't just abandon the project now."

"We're not abandoning it," Chip replied, running his thumb along the edge of the satellite phone, his eyes fixed on the blue tarp fluttering overhead where a roof should be. "We're recognizing that some things are more important than research schedules. These people welcomed us into their homes, homes that now barely exist. Our fish habitats can wait until they have places to sleep again."

21

STRAITS OF FLORIDA

The flight back to Florida was subdued. As the seaplane lifted off from Andros, Chip watched the island shrink beneath them, its green interior still beautiful despite the coastal devastation. He thought about the fishermen who would spend the next year rebuilding their boats, the families who would sleep under tarps until new roofs could be constructed, the community that had welcomed three strangers and trusted them with their most precious resource, their children's future.

"We'll be back," Tanner said, as if reading his thoughts.

"Yeah," Chip agreed, watching the turquoise water of the Tongue of the Ocean pass beneath them again. "But next time, we'll be better prepared."

As the Florida coast came into view, Chip felt a complex mixture of relief and guilt.

Relief to be returning to familiar territory, to problems that seemed manageable by comparison, but guilt at leaving behind people who had invested so much hope in their project, only to see it literally blown away by forces beyond anyone's control.

The seaplane touched down at Port Everglades just as the sun was setting, painting the sky in shades of orange and fuchsia that reminded Chip of his mornings at the beach house. Aunt Kim was waiting with her shiny, silver Range Rover, and just like old times, everything felt right. As they loaded their salt-stained equipment, Chip, Jake, and Tanner realized how much they'd missed the simple pleasure of being home. Even at their age, it was still very comforting to be picked up by family.

"So, what now?" Jake asked as they drove north toward Pelican Pointe.

"Now we figure out how to build hurricane-proof nursery habitats," Chip replied. "And we start raising money for the Andros reconstruction. Real reconstruction, not just our project, but the whole community."

"You think they'll want us back after this?" Tanner asked.

"Hopefully, but I have a feeling we're going to have our hands full here at home."

At that moment, Chip's phone buzzed with a text from his father: "Need to talk when you get home. Uncle Marcus's project is causing problems, AGAIN! Community meeting tonight."

Chip showed the text to his cousins and groaned. Chip looked at cousins, then Aunt Kim as she was driving. "Looks like we're not getting a break after all."

The three cousins exchanged glances. They'd spent months learning to navigate the politics of international conservation in foreign countries, but somehow dealing with family drama always felt way more complicated. The skills they'd developed in fishing villages and tourist destinations were about to be tested in the most challenging environment of all, their own community.

"At least this time we know what we're doing," Jake said, trying to sound optimistic.

"Do we though?" Chip muttered, watching the familiar Florida landscape roll past. "I mean, we couldn't even keep some floating habitats from getting destroyed by a hurricane."

"That wasn't our fault," Tanner said firmly. "Nature's gonna do what nature does. But this thing with Dad? That's just people being people. And we've gotten pretty good at handling people."

22

HOMECOMING HOOK

The Hillsboro Mile community center had never seen a crowd quite like the one that packed its old Dade pine-paneled meeting room that evening. On one side sat the usual suspects, wealthy retirees in tennis whites and golf shirts, clutching property deeds and architectural plans. On the other side, a group that would have seemed impossible just months earlier: members of the Miccosukee tribe in traditional dress, environmental activists with "Save Our Wetlands" signs, and a handful of marine biology students from the University of Miami. It was great to see Sloan again! Yep, she was there with the UM marine dream team.

And in the middle of it all sat Chip Waverly, still wearing his "Better in the Bahamas" t-shirt, feeling like he'd stepped through a portal into an alternate universe.

At 21, he felt way too young to be dealing with this kind of community drama, but here he was anyway. His Uncle Marcus, his dad's younger brother who'd always been the smooth-talking businessman of the family, commanded attention from the front of the room. Even in his expensive suit with that practiced smile, Chip could see the nervous energy radiating from his every gesture.

"Ladies and gentlemen, I want to assure everyone that Waverly Development has followed every regulation, dotted every i and crossed every t," Marcus was saying, his voice just a little too loud. "This project will bring jobs, increase property values, and showcase the very best of Florida luxury living."

An exhausted Tanner stood up to speak to his father. "Dad, our team has been talking to other tribes throughout Florida while we've been gone. There's growing interest in partnering with developers who respect their heritage and the land, but it has to be genuine partnership, not just consultation. Seriously, why can't we be that? You did it before, you can do it again!"

Marcus agreed to listen to his son, and over the next three hours, an extraordinary plan took shape. Instead of luxury condos that ignored the natural landscape, they revisited and envisioned an eco-resort that celebrated it: elevated buildings that allowed water flow beneath them, native plant landscaping that supported local wildlife, marina facilities designed to minimize impact on marine ecosystems.

"The profit margins might actually be higher," Jake noted, reviewing their financial projections. "Eco-tourism is a premium market, and this would be the first truly sustainable luxury development in South Florida."

However, persuading Uncle Marcus would demand more than just solid concepts, Chip realized. It would mean facing the investors who had already backed the original project, many of whom were known for their resistance to changes. So much had transpired during the boys' absence that the situation was nearly unrecognizable. Yet, they had navigated similar challenges before, and they could certainly do it again.

The confrontation came sooner than expected. Later that week, as Chip was presenting the alternative development plan to his family at the house, three black SUVs pulled through the gate into their circular driveway. The men who emerged wore expensive suits but carried themselves like people accustomed to getting their way through intimidation rather than negotiation. They went up the stairs of the beach home to the larger-than-life stained-glass doors that stood 15' high. Marcus could see through the pane of glass and opened the one door with hesitation.

"Marcus," the lead man said right away, "we hear there's been some discussion about changing our project. I want to make sure you understand that we have contracts, and we expect them to be honored."

Uncle Marcus's face had gone pale whilst still standing in the doorway. He asked the darkly dressed men to come in. "Vincent, these are just preliminary discussions. Nothing's been decided."

Chip had heard about Vincent Morrison from family conversations. He was the primary investor in Uncle Marcus's development project, the kind of guy who made money by buying up coastal land and turning it into luxury condos. Not exactly the type who cared about environmental impact.

But Chip stepped forward anyway, his six months of conservation work having taught him that some battles couldn't be avoided. Chip emerged from the large, lowered family room to come face to face with the man. "Mr. Morrison, I'm Marcus's nephew. I'd like to show you some projections that might interest you."

What followed was the most intense negotiation of

Chip's young life. Chip walked the group down to the drawing room where he presented financial models based on sustainable development, facts that showed they could actually increase profits while reducing legal risks. Jake backed him up with technical data about storm surge protection and environmental compliance, while Tanner used his natural charm to keep the conversation from turning into threats.

The breakthrough came when Dr. Blackwater, who rushed over when Chip texted her about this impromptu meeting, mentioned that the federal government was preparing to announce major tax incentives for developments that met certain environmental criteria and used blue economy ideas.

"Your original project would miss those incentives entirely," she told Morrison, "but this alternative approach would qualify for substantial federal and state benefits."

Morrison's demeanor shifted as he realized the financial implications. "How substantial are we talking?"

"Potentially fifteen to twenty percent of total project costs," Dr. Blackwater replied, pulling out documentation, "plus, long-term revenue streams from eco-tourism that could continue indefinitely."

By midnight, they had reached an agreement in principle. The Morrison Development project would be redesigned as a sustainable eco-resort, with the Miccosukee tribe as cultural partners, and environmental groups as ongoing advisors. Construction would begin in six months, allowing time for proper planning and community input.

Chip and his family walked the Morrison team to the towering front doors they first entered from, and said their goodbyes. He couldn't help but notice that 3 pelicans had landed on top of their SUVs, seemingly awaiting the results of the meeting. He could have sworn one gave him a wink before they flew away, as if they knew the trouble had been worked out.

As the men drove off into the night, Uncle Marcus put his arm around Chip's shoulders. "I don't know how you guys pulled that off, but you just saved our family's reputation and probably our business... again."

23

NEW RECRUITS

The three cousins had developed a tradition of meeting on Sunday mornings at the dock on Wahoo Bay Island, where they would each take out one of the research kayaks and paddle through the restored channels. They would pull up to an empty beach on the island, and sit to discuss anything and everything. These quiet moments on the water had become their time to reflect on everything they had learned and experienced together.

"Remember when we thought conservation was just about telling people what not to do?" Tanner asked one morning as they glided past a rookery where dozens of birds nested in the mangroves and pines. "Now I realize it's really about helping people find better ways to do what they need to do."

Chip ran his fingers through the warm sand, a satisfied grin spreading across his face. "I can't believe we actually pulled that off," he said, shaking his head in amazement.

Jake stretched out at the shoreline, his usually serious demeanor replaced by an expression of pure contentment. "My mom always said that when you do something good for others, the universe has a way of rewarding you," he mused, watching the waves lap gently at the shore. "I wonder what's coming next for us."

Tanner, ever the optimist, jumped to his feet and brushed the sand from his shorts. "I think we should start talking about going back to Andros and finish what we started, that would be incredible," he declared, his eyes sparkling with anticipation. "We make a pretty good team, don't we? But we need more of us if this is going to be sustainable and keep both communities operating."

All three Waverly boys agreed they needed some new recruits before they could embark on their return to Andros. They committed to spending time training a new group of young conservationists at Wahoo Bay. Twelve teenagers from across South Florida had been selected for the program, and Chip was amazed by their enthusiasm and fresh perspectives. They took notes from their friends at Bimini Shark Lab and environmental heroes over at Captains for Clean Water.

"The biggest thing we learned is you gotta listen first," Jake told the group during their first week of training. "Every community has its own story, you know? Their own problems, their own ways of dealing with stuff. We're not there to be like, 'Hey, we're the experts, do what we say.' We're there to help people figure out what actually works for them."

Tanner had put together this whole presentation about working with different cultures, based on everything they'd learned from Dr. Blackwater and the Miccosukee community as well as the warm, shining people of the Bahamas. "It's not just about being polite or whatever," he explained to the trainees. "It's about realizing that these communities have been taking care of their land way longer than we've even been alive. Like, thousands of years longer. We're the ones who need to learn from them, not the other way around."

As Chip observed the eager faces of the new young conservationists, their eyes wide with curiosity and determination, he felt a profound sense of satisfaction swell within him. Each lesson they absorbed was like a drop of water creating ripples in a still pond, spreading outward and gaining momentum. Their passion for the environment and commitment to conservation were not just fleeting moments; they were igniting a movement that would extend far beyond their own individual efforts, influencing communities and ecosystems in ways he could only begin to imagine.

24

THE RECOGNITION

The letter showed up on a Tuesday morning, hand delivered to the house. Chip stared at the official UN seal on the envelope, his hands actually shaking a little as he tore it open. Like, who gets mail from the United Nations?

"Guys," he called out from the back door of the kitchen that opens out to the pool, to Jake and Tanner, who were at the beach house on Hillsboro Mile. They were enjoying some much-needed pool time. "You need to see this."

The letter was an invitation to present their work at the UN Ocean Conference in Lisbon, Portugal.

Their Wahoo Bay project had been selected as one of twelve innovative conservation initiatives to be showcased before delegates from 193 countries.

"They want us to speak at the United Nations?" Jake asked, reading over Chip's shoulder. "About our little Florida project?"

"It's not little anymore," Tanner pointed out, gesturing toward his room with the wall where they'd mounted a map showing all their active sites. Red pins marked artificial reefs, blue pins showed nursery habitats, and green pins indicated community partnerships. The map looked like a constellation of conservation success stories stretching from the Florida Keys to the Bahamas.

Dr. Blackwater called, her usual composed demeanor replaced by barely contained excitement. "Did you see the news? The European Union just announced they're adopting your artificial reef design as their standard for marine habitat restoration. Looks like 'The Wahoo Bay Protocol' will be used throughout the Mediterranean and beyond!"

The recognition was overwhelming. Within a week, they received calls from marine conservation groups in Australia, Thailand, and Costa Rica, all wanting to implement similar programs. A documentary crew from National Geographic arrived to film their work, and Chip found himself being interviewed by reporters who seemed amazed that such a comprehensive conservation program had been developed by such a young group.

"The secret," Chip explained to the attentive journalist from Scientific American, his voice steady and filled with conviction, "is that we never forgot we were fishermen first. Every decision we make, every innovation we pursue, must resonate with the very people who rely on these waters for their livelihoods. We ensure that our methods are not just theoretical, but rooted in the practical realities faced by those who cast their nets and haul in the day's catch."

25

THE EXPANSION

By the conclusion of their fourth year, or their second year as an incorporated entity, Pelican Partners had transformed from three cousins attempting to save a few pelicans, into a legitimate conservation organization boasting numerous full-time staff, along with members and projects in three different countries. Their achievements on Andros had played a crucial role in solidifying the project. Occasionally, Chip would find himself in their new headquarters, reflecting on how they had evolved from rescuing a single bird sanctuary, to employing a dedicated team and forming international partnerships. It felt somewhat surreal. Their accomplishments had drawn significant funding from foundations and government agencies, but they also brought about new challenges.

"We need to be careful not to lose what made us successful in the first place," Chip warned during a staff meeting at their new headquarters, a converted warehouse over in Fort Lauderdale's Marina Mile that overlooked the Intracoastal Waterway. "The moment we start thinking like bureaucrats instead of fishermen, we'll lose our edge."

Jake had become their chief engineer, self taught, he was designing increasingly sophisticated habitat structures that could be manufactured and deployed anywhere in the world. His latest creation was a modular reef system that could be assembled underwater like an aquatic LEGO set, allowing local communities to customize their installations based on specific needs and conditions.

Tanner had evolved into their cultural liaison specialist, spending months at a time living with fishing communities in remote locations, learning their traditions and helping them adapt conservation techniques to their unique circumstances. His latest assignment had taken him to Belize, where he was working with traditional fishermen to restore coral reefs damaged by dynamite fishing.

"The principles are always the same," he reported

during a video call from a small cay southeast of Belize City. "Respect the local knowledge, provide economic alternatives, and make conservation profitable. But the details change completely depending on the culture and ecosystem."

Chip had discovered that his real talent lay in connecting different groups and finding common ground between seemingly incompatible interests. He'd become skilled at translating between the languages of science, business, and community activism, helping forge partnerships that none of the individual groups could have achieved alone.

Their remarkable success had woven a rich tapestry of connection with their families, bringing them full circle in a profound way. Uncle Marcus's eco-resort, a stunning fusion of nature and luxury, had blossomed into a shining model for sustainable development, garnering prestigious awards and drawing visitors from distant corners of the globe eager to witness how opulent tourism could harmoniously coexist with the protection of the environment. The Miccosukee partnership had flourished into a vibrant, comprehensive cultural education program, employing dozens of proud tribal members as passionate guides and educators, sharing their heritage with eager learners.

Meanwhile, the boys made frequent returns to the Bahamas. With their new team, and better technology, they made their way back not only to Andros, but installed far-improved floating nurseries around many of the other Bahamian islands. Bonefish Charlie said, "De nets ben filled with fish like dem old days." Dr. Rolle also expressed her gratitude, and told the boys they were an honorary part of the Bahamian family. Within months, the Bahamas had reclaimed its distinguished position on the world stage, celebrated once more for its unparalleled quality of fish and succulent lobster, a testament to both its natural bounty and the dedication of those who worked to preserve it.

26

THE FUTURE

On a warm evening in late spring, the three cousins found themselves back where it all started, sitting on the dock on Wahoo Bay Island, looking at the inlet, and watching the sunset paint the sky in brilliant cotton candy colors. The water around them teemed with life that hadn't been there four years earlier, and the sound of jumping fish created a constant symphony of splashes and ripples.

"You know what's crazy?" Jake said. "We literally started out just trying to help some birds, and somehow we ended up, I don't know, changing how people live? Like, actually changing how people think about this whole conservation thing."

Tanner nodded, watching an osprey hovering and hunting overhead, just waiting for a fish to appear from their first artificial reef that now hosted dozens of species under water.

Chip smiled, feeling the weight of everything they'd accomplished and everything still ahead of them. "The best part is, we're just getting started. There are a thousand more Wahoo Bays out there, waiting for someone to care enough to make a difference."

As the last golden hues of magic hour melted into a green flash on the horizon, a familiar sound resonated across the shimmering water: the distinctive, resonant call of a brown pelican. The trio lifted their gazes to witness a majestic brown pelican soaring gracefully, leading a V formation of younger birds gliding effortlessly toward their evening roost, wings outstretched against the twilight sky.

The Waverly boys lounged in a chill silence, the soft sound of waves crashing nearby creating a laid-back vibe as they mulled over their thoughts. They knew tomorrow would bring new challenges, exciting chances, and plenty of ways to show that conservation wasn't just about saving nature; it was a real promise to build a better future for everyone living on this awesome blue planet. The air buzzed with anticipation, and the salty scent of the ocean mixed with the thrill of what was to come.

The Problem with Pelicans is based on true happenings in South Florida in the early 2000's.

The narrative of Pelican Pointe and The Wahoo Bay Restoration Project is fictional, yet we aim to illustrate that young individuals need not wait to become adults to significantly impact environmental conservation. In South Florida, teenagers organize a multitude of beach cleanups that remove thousands of pounds of plastic waste each year, collaborating with marine biology labs to gather water quality data, and even speaking before city councils to advocate for stronger environmental protections. The crucial factor was finding ways to channel their youthful energy and idealism into practical skills with mentorship from adults.

Whether it involved learning to identify invasive species in local parks, assisting elderly neighbors in installing rain gardens to mitigate stormwater runoff, or utilizing social media to raise awareness among their peers about sustainable practices, young conservationists were realizing that environmental stewardship began right in their own neighborhoods. The most successful youth programs integrated hands-on outdoor experiences with real-world problem solving, equipping teenagers with the tools and confidence to emerge as environmental leaders in their communities rather than mere bystanders to ecological degradation.

The Artificial Reef Systems mentioned in the story are a very real thing, and have revolutionized marine conservation by creating a practical solution that benefits both environmental and economic interests, thus, making conservation financially sustainable for local communities. The system's success in supporting fish breeding and population recovery has made it a model for global marine restoration efforts. Its modular design allows communities to start small and expand based on their needs and resources, making marine conservation more accessible to developing coastal regions. The technology has become a cornerstone of modern marine ecosystem restoration, demonstrating how engineered solutions can support natural processes while maintaining economic viability.

You can explore the vibrant opportunities that await you right in your own community. If you are in a coastal town, please check with your chamber of commerce and social media. There is a treasure trove of marine volunteer work opportunity. Immerse yourself in the rich tapestry of activities and connections that foster a sense of belonging and excitement right outside your front door.

A special thank you to my friends and family for all the inspiration on this project.

RESOURCES

As you just read in the book, here are three very real organizations you can get involved with, or just keep up with all the amazing work they do!

Captains for Clean Water
https://captainsforcleanwater.org

Bimini Shark Lab
https://biminisharklab.com

Ocean Rescue Alliance International
https://oceanrescuealliance.org

You can also find out more about the history of the Miccosukee Tribe at
https://miccosukee.com/miccosukee-tribe-history

ABOUT THE AUTHOR

Meet Ms. Maudie Lancaster! A South Florida native, ocean biologist, ecologist, and passionate fisherman, Ms. Maudie loves exploring the Atlantic Ocean's beauty. Through her characters' adventures, she teaches young readers about the importance of caring for our oceans, protecting marine life, and understanding ecological science. With a love for fishing and nature, she hopes her stories inspire everyone to help save the ocean, and keep its wonders alive for generations to come!